CHRISTMAS COVER-UP

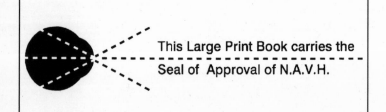

This Large Print Book carries the
Seal of Approval of N.A.V.H.

FAMILY REUNION SERIES

CHRISTMAS COVER-UP

LYNETTE EASON

THORNDIKE PRESS

A part of Gale, Cengage Learning

GALE
CENGAGE Learning·

Farmington Hills, Mich • San Francisco • New York • Waterville, Maine
Meriden, Conn • Mason, Ohio • Chicago

Copyright © 2013 by Lynette Eason.
Family Reunion Series #2
Thorndike Press, a part of Gale, Cengage Learning.

LIBRARY OF CONGRESS CATALOGING-IN-PUBLICATION DATA

Eason, Lynette.
   Christmas cover-up / by Lynette Eason. — Large Print edition.
      pages cm. — (Family Reunion series ; #2) (Thorndike Press Large Print Christian Mystery)
   ISBN-13: 978-1-4104-6744-7 (hardcover)
   ISBN-10: 1-4104-6744-9 (hardcover)
   1. Kidnapping—Fiction. 2. Cold cases (Criminal investigation)—Fiction. 3. Christmas stories. 4. Large type books. I. Title.
   PS3605.A79C47 2014
   813'.6—dc23
                                   2013047775

Published in 2014 by arrangement with Harlequin Books S.A.

Printed in Mexico
1 2 3 4 5 6 7 18 17 16 15 14

For it is by grace you have been saved, through faith — and this is not from yourselves, it is the gift of God.

— *Ephesians* 2:8

To my Lord and Savior, who loves me unconditionally and died so I could live.

Thanks to my ACFW Suspense Loop friends for your brainstorming help on this series. So many great ideas and suggestions went into this story. Couldn't have done it without you!

ONE

Keys clutched in her left hand, Detective Katie Randall stared at her vandalized front door. She hadn't noticed it when she'd pulled into the drive; she'd been too busy thinking about her sister's cold case and the man who'd been assigned to help her work on it. Lucy had disappeared fourteen years ago from her front yard and it was time Katie and her family found closure.

Now she'd come home to this.

She'd parked in the drive and grabbed her stuff from the car, still thinking about canceling the meeting she had coming up in about five minutes.

It was only when she'd gotten closer to the house that she'd seen the splintered wood around the doorknob. And the Christmas wreath lying on the porch.

The hair on the nape of her neck spiked, and she stepped back. She set her briefcase and keys on the porch. The chilly December wind found its way under her collar, and she shivered as she mentally flipped through her options at lightening speed.

Her nerves tightened, muscles bunched. She pulled her weapon from her shoulder holster as she backed down the steps of the porch. With her left hand, she snagged her cell phone from the back pocket of her khaki slacks and pressed the speed dial number for Jordan Gray, the man she was supposed to meet in less than five minutes. She couldn't let him walk into a potentially dangerous situation without some warning.

He answered on the third ring. "Almost there."

"Don't pull in the drive. Someone's either been in my house or is still there."

"Give me thirty seconds."

"I'm calling for backup. I'll be inside. Mariah might be here and need help."

Mariah Sims, Katie's friend and roommate. Mariah usually got home before Katie.

She hung up on his protests and orders to wait for him. Hesitating, she debated whether or not to call her partner, Gregory Lee, but decided Jordan, a former FBI agent, would be able to handle this just as well as Gregory.

And he was closer. She dialed 911 and

within seconds had backup on the way. Once the address went out, every officer within a ten-mile radius would be on her doorstep.

She made her way up the porch steps again. Christmas lights lined the railing. Katie stood to the side of the broken door and nudged it open. "Mariah? Are you here?"

Silence greeted her call.

Katie whispered up a silent prayer for Mariah's safety.

She glanced over her shoulder as Jordan's car edged to the curb in front of her neighbor's home. He climbed out, weapon in his hand as he jogged over to stand beside her. She'd hired him through Finding the Lost to locate her missing sister. The Finding the Lost organization, founded by skip-tracer Erica James, specialized in locating missing people. From private investigators to contracted FBI agents to police detectives, a plethora of talented men and woman worked tirelessly to help others reunite with lost loved ones.

Katie had hired the organization and then had second thoughts about doing so when she discovered who would handle her case. Jordan Gray. She knew him slightly because of her connection to Erica, his boss, but hadn't realized Neil Gray was his brother. The brother who'd been killed in a jail cell after Katie arrested him for drunk driving.

Before she had a chance to tell Jordan she'd decided she couldn't work with him, he'd called fifteen minutes ago to let her know he was on the way to her house.

He was ambushing her and she hadn't been able to put him off. Now she was glad for his presence. She gestured to the open door. "Will you cover me?"

He didn't waste time chastising her for not waiting on him. "What's the layout?"

"Foyer leads straight into the great room. Two bedrooms and a bath to the right, kitchen and dining to the left. My bedroom is also to the left behind the garage."

"I'll go right, you go left."

Katie stepped into her house and caught her breath. Chaos greeted her. Cushions pulled off her couch and slashed. Bookcase overturned and coffee table shoved on its side. The Christmas tree she and Mariah had decorated lay on its side, ornaments crushed from one end of the room to the other.

A thud from the back of the house caused her to stiffen and shoot a glance at Jordan. "You hear that?" she whispered.

"Yeah. Where'd it come from?" He kept

his voice low.

"I don't know."

"Is your roommate here?"

"She usually parks in the garage, but I don't know if her car's in there or not." She would have checked before entering the house, but the windows for the garage had blinds on them. And they were closed.

Katie moved farther inside, sidestepping the mess. Jordan went right, weapon in front of him.

Katie passed the open-area kitchen on her left, rounded the breakfast bar and stepped into the hallway. To her left was the utility room, to the right the half bath and the exit to the back porch that ran the length of the house.

The half bath sat empty. All that was left was her room and bath. Her room looked like the great room area: destroyed.

She ignored the anger at the invasion and headed back to join Jordan.

"Freeze! FBI!"

Katie did for a brief second before she realized the yell wasn't aimed at her.

A crash. Running footsteps.

A dark-clothed figure raced past the doorway where she stood and into Mariah's bedroom, with Jordan on his heels. Katie bolted after them.

The intruder leaped over the bed and wrenched the French doors open. Jordan followed and Katie turned to race from the bedroom, back into the great room and out onto the back porch.

The French doors swung open and the figure halted when he realized Katie had him cut off. She pointed her weapon. "Freeze! Police!"

He obeyed for a millisecond, then vaulted over the railing. Again Jordan followed while Katie spun and took the steps two at a time to the yard, where Jordan tackled the man. Sirens screaming, three cruisers pulled up to the curb.

Jordan ducked as a fist swung around toward his face. As the intruder's punch met air, Jordan pulled back his right arm and let his knuckles crunch against the guy's jaw. Dazed, the fight drained from the man, and he lay on his back panting, glaring as the sting of the hit faded.

With her gun in her right hand, Katie used her left to toss a pair of handcuffs to Jordan.

"Let us know if you need help."

Jordan looked up to see three officers, guns drawn, ready to jump in. He sucked in a lungful of air. "I think we got it."

Katie walked over and continued to cover the man until Jordan had him on his stomach, hands cuffed behind his back. "You have the right to remain silent . . ." Katie read him his rights as Jordan patted the man down. Finding no weapon, he rose to his feet.

When she was finished, she looked at the officers. "This will just take a minute, then he's all yours. She shoved her intruder over to the steps of the porch. "Sit."

Jordan watched the man obey. Reluctantly and with narrowed green eyes that glinted with anger.

Katie looked at Jordan. "You're not FBI. Why'd you identify yourself as such?"

He felt a flush start at the base of his neck. Then gave a small shrug even as the shadows danced across his mind. He pushed them away. "I am again as of last month. Simply doing some consulting work with them."

"Oh."

He spread his hands, palms up. "They asked."

"Right. Well, that should make my lieutenant happier." Jordan knew her lieutenant hadn't been too keen on Katie having access to her sister's files, but he had finally caved, especially when she'd explained that she was hiring an outside organization to help. He'd been intrigued by the idea and finally agreed as long as she kept him updated. And worked the case on her own time. As far as Jordan could tell, she'd kept to that promise.

She stared at him a moment longer, then turned her frown at her intruder. "Who are you, and what were you doing in my house?"

His gaze lowered to the badge on her belt. "You're a cop?"

"I am."

"And you're FBI?" He directed his question to Jordan, who gave a sharp nod.

"Figures." He clamped his lips and looked away. Jordan decided the guy was younger than he'd originally thought. Maybe in his mid-twenties.

"Your name?" Katie demanded.

"Wesley Wray."

"What were you looking for, Mr. Wray?" Jordan asked.

Wesley shrugged. "Whatever I could find. Jewelry, cash, whatever."

Katie snapped his picture with her iPhone and emailed it directly to her office with instructions to find out everything possible about this man. "So this was just a random thing? You picked my house out of all the ones in this subdivision?"

"Yeah, I guess. It looked like an easy hit." He shook his head and muttered, "Didn't know you were a cop."

Jordan saw skepticism skitter across Katie's face and knew she wasn't buying the guy's story. Jordan hauled the man to his feet. "Come on, you can tell the rest of this sad tale downtown."

As he stood, Wesley's gaze landed on Katie's briefcase sitting on the front porch. "Your laptop in there?"

She frowned. "It is. Why?"

"Nothing."

Jordan led Wesley to a waiting police cruiser. Jordan recognized Chris Jiles as one of the officers. Chris locked his hand around Wray's upper arm and looked at Katie. "You all right?"

"Never better."

"Right." He helped Jordan get Mr. Wray secured in the back of the cruiser. She walked over and shook hands with Chris. "I'll be down to the station shortly to fill out a report. Stick him in one of the interrogation rooms and let him sit for a bit."

"Will do. You need a crime scene unit?"

"Why? We caught him red-handed and he confessed. Let's not waste lab dollars on a simple B & E."

He shrugged. "Your call."

Chris drove off with his prisoner, followed by the other officers who'd shown up. Katie turned to Jordan.

Dressed in pressed khaki pants and a blue button-up shirt, she had her straight blond hair pulled back in a ponytail with a plain band. Her light brown eyes still glinted steel. A faint dusting of freckles and no makeup would make a lot of women look plain. Katie, however, was a natural beauty.

He ignored the zing of attraction he always seemed to get around her and followed her up the front porch steps.

Romance, attraction, whatever it was he felt when he spent time with her was not an option. Katie Randall had killed his brother — at least in his parents' eyes — and while he'd work with her on this case, getting personal was out of the question. And besides, she'd gone out her way to avoid him ever since she'd learned he would be the one handling the case.

They stepped back inside and the destruction greeted them.

Even though she'd already seen it, he heard her suck in a deep breath and let it out slowly. "Looks like you're going to have your hands full cleaning this up."

She sighed. "Looks like. Fifteen days until Christmas and this. Lovely. Just what I wanted to come home to." She grimaced. "Okay, I'll stop whining now. Sorry."

He gave a short laugh. "I'll help."

Really? And why was he offering to spend more time with her than necessary? She lifted a brow. "I'll probably call a cleaning crew, but thanks."

Relieved — yet strangely disappointed — he nodded and looked around. "Mariah's not here, obviously."

"No." She walked into the kitchen and looked out the window into the garage. "Her car's not here. She either stayed late at work or stopped somewhere on her way home."

Jordan tilted his head toward the back of the house. "Your office is trashed, too."

Katie spun on her heel and walked to her office. *Trashed* was a kind word. "He asked about my laptop. Do you find that strange?"

"Yes. A bit."

Katie walked to Mariah's room. Mariah had gone crazy with Christmas decorations. Decorations that were still in their place, none broken, none touched. Jordan followed. She said, "But he didn't touch anything in here."

"Maybe he just didn't have time to get to it."

"Maybe."

"Or he was just interested in your stuff and not hers."

"But why? And why ask about my laptop?"

"I think we'll have to get Mr. Wray to answer those questions."

Katie rubbed her head, hoping the action would push away the building headache. "I guess this means our meeting is on hold."

"Again."

Katie felt a flush of guilt stain her cheeks. It was true. She'd been putting him off, delaying their getting together. Every time she was around him, she expected him to bring up his brother. And her part in the man's death. Her avoidance of Jordan was unusual. Normally if she needed to address something unpleasant, she did it and got it over with. Not so with this man. "It's not like I planned this."

"No, but you've been avoiding meeting with me. You're the one who came to us, remember? I've been working this case for the past two weeks. I need you to be available to answer questions when they come up. By putting me off, you're making it exceedingly difficult for me to do my job." He studied her. "And after you went to all that trouble to convince your lieutenant to grant us access to files and everything related to Lucy's case."

Katie grimaced at the memory of going to her lieutenant and unashamedly begging him to allow them to do this. "I know. I know," she groaned. "He really didn't want to, but he likes me. Although he did warn me that if this came back to bite him, I'd be checking parking meters until I retired." She rubbed her eyes. "It'll help that you're back with the FBI. He's not like some who get defensive about territory. He welcomes any help he can get."

A faint smile crossed his face, then faded. "Is your reluctance because of Neil?"

Katie stared at him, taken aback by his bluntness. Then a small kernel of anger formed in her belly. She curled her fingers into fists then had to make a concentrated effort to relax. It wasn't his fault she didn't want to talk to him. Not totally, anyway. "Yes, it's partly because of Neil. I didn't really expect Erica to give this case to you." Erica James, the director of Finding the Lost, was one of Katie's closest friends. "She knows what happened with Neil and — and I just —" She broke off and swallowed hard. "Although I suppose it makes the most sense with your FBI connections." She frowned. "I can drive."

"That's all right, I don't mind. Where will

21

you and Mariah stay until you get this cleaned up?"

"Good question." Relieved not to talk about his brother just yet, Katie pulled her phone out and started to dial Mariah's number when she heard a car pull into the drive. She walked out onto the front porch to see her roommate climb from her vehicle.

Mariah spotted Jordan and waved. "Hey, you two, what's going on?" Jordan and Mariah had met once when Jordan had come by to pick up information regarding her sister's kidnapping.

"We had a break-in," Katie said.

Mariah's pretty green eyes went wide. "A break-in? Are you all right?"

"Yes," Katie assured her, then explained what had happened. "But it's pretty bad inside. I think we need to find another place to stay until a cleaning crew can come out here." She paused. "Although your room looks fine. He didn't get that far."

Jordan said, "He just raced out the French doors. But your stuff didn't look touched."

Mariah bit her lip and tucked a stray hunk of chocolate-brown hair behind her ear. "You think he'll come back?"

"No, we caught him. But the kitchen and den area aren't livable right now. He slashed the cushions and —"

Mariah rushed past her and into the house. Her outraged cry made Katie grimace. Her roommate raced to Katie's bedroom, then the office and finally her own bedroom. Tears stood in her friend's eyes. "I don't want to stay here. And you can't. He slashed up your mattress."

"I know."

Mariah took a deep breath. "We'll stay with Grandma Jean. She has that big ol' house with plenty of room. She'd love it if we crashed there for a few days."

Katie smiled as she thought of the spry eighty-year-old woman who still lived life to the fullest. "All right, you ask her. I've got to get down to the station and question our intruder."

Mariah shuddered. "I can't believe someone would break into a cop's house."

Katie shrugged. "I don't think he knew I was a cop." She frowned. "I can't help thinking this isn't a random break-in."

Mariah fished in her large shoulder bag and produced her phone. "I'll throw some things in a bag and call Grandma Jean and tell her we're coming."

Katie looked at Jordan. "Guess I'll do the same, then we can go. I'll take my car and you can ride with me if you want. Mariah's grandmother only lives about a mile from here, so I can bring you back here to get your car before I go over there for the night."

"That sounds good."

Katie smiled then walked into her destroyed bedroom. The smile slipped away and anger swept over her, hot and swift even as she gave thanks that Mariah hadn't been here when the intruder broke in. She grabbed an overnight bag and threw some items in it, including work clothes for the next day. She then examined every inch of her bedroom even though she knew Wray hadn't taken anything. Her jewelry box lay open, but nothing was missing.

A shudder of revulsion went through her. She dealt with criminals every day. But she'd never had one in her house. Her bedroom. It made her skin crawl.

Katie spun toward the door, anxious to get out of the room, and ran into Mariah coming from her bedroom. Her friend said, "We're all set. Grandma Jean's excited to have company tonight."

"I'll call someone to come clean this up, and we'll put better locks on the doors." She paused. "And maybe an alarm system."

"All right. I'll see you later tonight, then."

Katie nodded and joined Jordan, who waited patiently in the den. "I'm ready."

He followed her outside and stopped at her vehicle. She opened her door and looked at him. He placed a hand over hers. The heat of his palm seeped through the back of her hand, warming her. "What is it?" When he hesitated, she took a deep breath. His spicy cologne filled the air. Katie told herself she had to ignore the fact that she found him attractive and focus on doing what they needed to do so they could part company. "Jordan?"

He said, "I know my parents blame you for Neil's death, but I didn't realize —"

She tensed. "What?"

"You blame yourself for my brother's death, too, don't you?"

Two

She climbed into the car and shut the door. Jordan walked around and did the same, wondering if she was going to answer him. Then she bit her lip and nodded. "Yes. He was just a kid." She cranked the car and backed out of the drive.

"You were doing your job."

"I know that," she snapped. Then took a deep breath. "Sorry."

"It's okay. Neil was at a party and he'd been drinking. He decided to drive home rather than be smart and call someone to pick him up."

"What male is smart at the age of twenty?"

A short, humorless laugh barked from him. "None. Not a single one."

"But he shouldn't have died because he was just stupid."

"No, he shouldn't have."

She drew in a deep breath. "I didn't know what would happen. I let him make a phone call and put him in the holding cell. Then I went to do the paperwork and about an hour later —"

"I know."

"There were so many arrests that night," she whispered. "It was crazy."

"It was New Year's Eve. It's always like that."

"There was no choice but to fill the holding cells up."

"Katie, you don't have to justify that night to me. I've worked law enforcement. I know what it's like." He swallowed hard and sighed. "You had no idea a meth head would kill two people with his bare hands before someone could get in there. You can't predict what's going to happen in those cells. Most of the time nothing does." His jaw tightened, and his eyes narrowed. "The fact is, if my brother hadn't chosen to be stupid, he'd still be alive."

His anger vibrated between them. He was still furious with Neil. But not with her. Not anymore. He looked at her and felt frustration swamp him when he couldn't read her expression. "So do you want me to quit looking into your sister's kidnapping or not?"

Katie bit her lip and glanced at him. "I don't know, but knowing you don't hold me responsible for Neil's death helps."

"I don't, but I'll be honest, my parents do and I'm afraid I'll never convince them otherwise."

She flinched and nodded.

He pinched the bridge of his nose. "You came to us."

"I know that."

He thought about all the work he'd already done, the people he'd questioned, the answers that produced more questions. "I can't do my job without your cooperation. Your sister's been missing for fourteen years. Do you want me to keep working on trying to find out what happened to her or not?" Trying to find a person missing for the past fourteen years was hard enough, but trying to find one without the cooperation of the one who'd hired him would be impossible.

"Yes. No." She hissed out a breath and tightened her fingers around the wheel. After she made a left turn, she said, "It's harder than I thought it would be."

"Why?"

"Because every time I look at you, I think of Neil. I think of your father in the morgue and his —" She bit her lip and looked away.

His phone rang and he snagged it, deciding to take the call and give her a bit of breathing room. "Hello?"

"Jordan. This is Erica."

"What can I do for you?"

"Have you had a chance to talk to Katie?" He and Erica had discussed Katie's reluctance to have him lead the investigation into her sister's disappearance.

"In the process now."

"Sorry, didn't mean to rush you. I'm just concerned."

"I know. I'll give you an update soon." He hung up and turned back to Katie. "That was Erica."

"Why did she assign my case to you?" Katie asked.

"Because I had just finished up with one and had the time to take it." He paused. "Did you tell her anything about our background?"

Katie shook her head.

"So she didn't know." He sighed. "Look. If you don't want me working it, I'll tell Erica. But you should know everyone is slammed right now. When Erica finally found Molly after three years and brought her home, those front-page headlines had people coming out of the woodwork. There are so many cold-case disappearances with desperate family members thinking Finding the Lost is their only hope. If you back off of Lucy's case now, it might be a while before someone else can pick it back up."

She drove without speaking until they were almost to the station. "I don't know if I can work with you. You're a constant reminder that I caused someone's death. How can you work with me day in and day out and not think about him? Not remember? Not feel some kind of anger toward me?" Her low voice reverberated with pain that echoed his own.

His heart hurt when he thought of his twenty-year-old brother. He'd been dead for a little over a year and the pain still cut sometimes.

Neil, the black sheep. The wild young man just sowing his oats. Neil, lying in the coffin because he'd chosen to drink and drive and then get stuck in a cell with the wrong person. Neil, whose dark secrets, known only to Jordan and the medical examiner, went to the grave with him, leaving Jordan with the burden of what to do with them. Especially the question of whether or not to tell his parents the truth about what really had been going on with Neil. Like his drug problem. "Neil doesn't have anything to do with me doing my job."

She pulled into the parking lot of the station and turned off the vehicle. She looked at him. "How can you be objective? Your brother is dead because I arrested him and stuck him in a cell with a crazy person. How can you not blame me, too?"

"For starters, you didn't know the guy was crazy. And second, my brother is dead because he made some really bad choices. I don't blame you, I blame Neil and the guy who killed him. Period. Those are the only two who deserve the blame."

"Like you said, your parents don't feel that way."

Jordan closed his eyes, remembering his father's confrontation of Katie at the morgue. Paul Gray had stared daggers at Katie. "You killed my son!"

Katie had winced and held out a hand. "I'm so sorry this happened. Neil ran a stop sign right in front of me. I pulled him over and he was —"

"You did this. You!" He'd jabbed a finger, stopping millimeters from her chest, cutting off her sorrowful words. "Neil called me. Said he didn't know why he'd been arrested, that it was a case of mistaken identity. You made a mistake, and an innocent boy died because of it. I hope you can sleep tonight knowing how well you did your duty." The thick sarcasm cut.

"Sir —"

His father had turned on his heel and marched away, never looking back. And Jordan had just stood there and let the man blast Katie. Then again, he'd wanted to do the same thing. Before he'd learned the truth about everything. That Neil was into drugs, buying, selling and using. And he was in deep.

The pain of that day swept over him once again.

The agony on Katie's face shook him. "He wasn't innocent like your parents believe, but Neil shouldn't have died because of that choice," she reiterated with a whisper.

"No, he shouldn't have." Jordan rubbed a hand down his face. "This is why you've been avoiding me?"

"Mostly."

He nodded. "All right. We've gotten this far in talking about it, but we'll have to finish this conversation later. Let's go see what our prisoner has to say."

Katie nodded and climbed from the car.

Katie stepped into the police station. Jordan nodded to an officer and said, "I want to speak to Kurt over there. His father and mine are friends. I'll be there in just a minute."

She nodded and took a right down a long

hallway. She stopped in front of a room labeled Interrogation Room #2 and took a deep breath.

Questioning a suspect always gave her an adrenaline rush. Mr. Wesley Wray was no different. She knew Jordan would be watching from the observation window. Katie stepped into the interrogation room and dropped a file on the table in front of Wray. She sat across from him and settled one hand on top of the file. His eyes followed her movement. She asked, "You've got quite a history of breaking into places, don't you?"

His gaze snapped up to meet hers. He narrowed his eyes, leaned back and crossed his arms. "So?"

She shrugged and kept her voice conversationally light. "What do you do when you're not in jail, Mr. Wray? Do you have a family?"

His brow furrowed. She'd confused him. "Yeah. I got a wife and a kid that live over behind the Beacon."

The Beacon. One of Spartanburg's most well-known landmarks. Anyone who came through the city as a tourist stopped to eat there. But one didn't want to live behind it. It was one of the toughest areas in town, where residents kept their doors locked and their weapons nearby.

"So I want to know, out of all the houses in Spartanburg, what made you pick mine?"

"I told you, Detective, it was empty and looked like an easy hit. I thought I'd be in and out before anyone got home. End of story."

She leaned in. "Oh, no. I think there's a lot more to that story than you're telling, and we're not going anywhere until I'm satisfied you've given me quite a few more details. Why did you ask about my laptop? Is there something on there you're interested in?"

For a brief second, Wray looked startled, a deer caught in the headlights, then he sneered and leaned forward, the tic alongside his mouth betraying his emotion. "Look, lady —"

"That's 'detective.' "

"Detective," Wray sneered. His face cleared, the tic stopped. "There's nothing else to tell. I needed some cash for a hit. Your house looked ripe."

Katie studied him. "You're not a junkie."

He lifted a brow and shrugged. "I didn't say the hit was for me."

She slammed a hand on the table and he jumped. "Quit playing me! What were you doing in my house?"

■ ■ ■ ■

Jordan shoved his hands in the pockets of his jeans. If he didn't, the temptation to burst into the investigation room and wrap his fingers around Wray's throat might just be too much for him.

He slid a glance at Gregory Lee, Katie's partner. The man had come when he'd heard the call over his radio. Jordan said, "She holds her own, doesn't she?"

"She's sharp. Can spot a lie a mile away. Only you know as well as I do she shouldn't be in there questioning him."

"I know. You going to get in there and tell her to get out?"

"In a minute or two."

Jordan smothered a smile. Gregory was a good partner. He stood about two inches over six feet, and Jordan knew he'd just celebrated his thirty-third birthday, because one of Katie's excuses for not meeting with him last week was because she had a birthday party to attend for her partner.

"You have any thoughts on why Wray would have been in Katie's house?"

Lee shook his head. "No."

"Any cases y'all are working bring anything to mind?"

Gregory finally looked at him. "Nothing in particular. Why? You don't think this was a random thing?"

"Do you?"

Gregory shrugged. "Cops don't have any special protection when it comes to a breaking and entering."

"I know. It just seems . . . odd. He breaks into her house at five-thirty on a Tuesday afternoon. That's about the time a lot of people are coming home from work. Why risk being spotted by a neighbor or the homeowner walking in on him . . . like Katie did."

"Good questions." Gregory eyed him. "Why don't you pass those on to Katie?"

"She'll think of them."

Katie looked up and scratched her nose.

Gregory said, "That's my cue." He breathed a sigh of relief. "She's not pushing. She's going to let me push the guy." He shot Jordan a look. "Guess I'll get to ask those questions." He slipped from the observation room and soon was in the interrogation room. Katie pressed the file into his hands and within seconds joined Jordan. "You look tired," he said.

"Tired and frustrated."

Jordan nodded. "I understand. But just one question."

"What's that?"

"If Wray didn't pick your home by accident, then what was the reason behind the break-in?"

"Exactly what I've been trying to figure out."

Unfortunately, Gregory didn't get anything else out of Mr. Wray, either, and they left with more questions than answers.

On the way to the car, she asked, "What are your plans tonight?"

"I'm going to stop at my parents' house, then head home. I need to go over some notes."

She cocked her head. "Do you work all the time?"

Jordan flashed her a tight smile. "Of course. Don't you?"

She blew out a short laugh. "Yeah. Pretty much." She paused and bit her lip.

"What is it?"

Katie sighed. "Are you going to tell your parents we're working together?"

Jordan pressed his lips together as he pondered that question. "I don't know."

She nodded, her eyes troubled. Jordan found himself wanting to soothe the agitation there. He wanted to take her in his arms and reassure her that it would be all right. He swallowed hard and resisted the desire to act on those feelings.

He pictured that day in the morgue. Looking down at his brother's face. Surrounded by his parents' grief and Katie's guilt-ridden eyes.

He shuddered. Yeah. Better to turn those feelings off now before they developed into something that would break both of their hearts.

THREE

Wednesday morning Katie woke to the sun streaming through the blinds and a headache she wouldn't wish on her worst enemy. Except maybe her uncooperative intruder from yesterday. Yeah. He could have it.

She squinted against the light and held a hand to her throbbing head, wondering who'd stabbed her just above her right eye. She glanced at the clock. Eight-fifteen. Where was she?

Oh, right, Grandma Jean's. And today was Wednesday. Grandma Jean would be at her weekly Bible study and Mariah, a crime-lab technician, would have left for work about thirty minutes ago.

Katie moved and the room tilted. She groaned and decided the pain felt like little men with ice picks were assaulting her head.

Medicine first.

Call in sick second.

Once she'd ticked both items off her list,

she closed the curtains over the blinds and crawled back under the covers. Bracing her head against the headboard, she kept her eyes shut and let her mind spin.

Time passed in a blur. It seemed like mere minutes when her cell phone rang, jarring her from her twilight sleep. A quick glance at the clock told her it was lunchtime. Her stomach growled in agreement.

She answered on the third ring. "Hello?"

"Katie? You all right?" Jordan asked.

She supposed her froglike voice might have clued him in that something might be wrong. "Yeah. Had a bad headache."

"Had? As in it's gone now?"

She considered the question. "Not entirely, but it's better. Manageable."

"Manageable enough to meet me for lunch?"

Did she want to? Not really, because she had a feeling what the topic of conversation would be. But she'd made this decision to pursue her sister's case. A case that wouldn't even exist if Katie hadn't turned her back on Lucy for just a little too long. Lucy had been seven years old when fourteen-year-old Katie had helped a neighbor with her groceries. When she'd returned to the yard, Lucy had been gone. And Katie had been blamed by her parents ever since. Especially

40

her mother.

It wasn't too late to back out, but she knew deep down she didn't want to do that. She needed to know what had happened to Lucy, needed somehow to absolve herself of this raging guilt she'd carried for the last fourteen years. "Sure. What'd you have in mind?"

"I think I remember you like pizza?"

"Of course."

"How about Gino's?"

The little pizza place about three minutes from Grandma Jean's house. She swiped a hand through her hair. "Give me about thirty minutes."

"Deal."

"And I'm paying for mine, okay? I mean, this isn't like a date, right?" she blurted. Silence from the other end. She fought the mortification at her silly assumption that he had even thought about paying for her lunch.

She opened her mouth to apologize only to hear him say on a choked laugh, "Well, if I'd been thinking along those lines, I'm not now."

"Sorry, sorry. I didn't mean to make things awkward. Was actually trying to avoid that by clearing that up before we met."

He gave another low chuckle and she

41

knew if she looked in the mirror, she'd be beet red. "You can pay for yours. See you soon, Katie." His silky goodbye sent shivers dancing up her spine. Oh, no. She had *not* just done that, had she? Why, oh why couldn't she just keep her mouth shut?

And yet she couldn't extinguish the spark of excitement that flared at the thought of being with him again. "It's not a date," she reminded herself as she flew through her routine, her headache all but gone.

Twenty-six minutes later, she walked through the door of the popular pizza café and spotted Jordan seated at a back table with a large pizza at the center. Christmas music played in the background, and a toasty fire added to the warmth of the atmosphere.

Katie slid into the chair opposite him. A glass of iced tea sat in front of her and she took a swig. He handed her a plate and a napkin. "Pepperoni all right?"

"More than all right. It's my favorite."

"That's what I've heard."

He had, huh? Erica?

She waited for him to mention her embarrassing moment on the phone, but he seemed to have let it go. She relaxed and for the next few minutes they ate while

Katie wondered about the man across from her.

"What's your story, Jordan?"

He stilled, glanced up at her then back to his pizza. "What do you mean?"

"You used to be with the FBI full time. Why did you leave to come work for Erica?"

"Partly because Brandon asked me to." Brandon Hayes was Erica's brother and partner with Finding the Lost. And Jordan's roommate. He chewed his food and swallowed. "It's a long story."

He obviously didn't want to talk about it, but she decided not to let him off the hook that easily. "I've got time." He knew her entire sordid mess of a story. Would he trust her enough to share his background?

He stared at her then looked down at his food. "I was working with the Crimes Against Children division. Fighting online predators. I messed up and a kid died. End of story."

Katie gasped. "Jordan, I'm so sorry."

He continued to eat in silence, but Katie knew there was more. She decided to go for broke. "How did you mess up?"

He paused, set the uneaten piece of pizza on his plate and sighed. "I was outsmarted."

She stared at him, skeptical. "I can't see that happening."

For a moment his eyes thawed and the grief that had been there faded a fraction. "Thanks for that." He shook his head. "The guy on the other end of the computer had routed his IP address through so many different places, I was having a hard time tracking him. When I finally got a lock on him, it was too late. He'd killed the young girl and taken off."

"Was he ever found?"

"Yes. The next day, when he tried to snatch another kid."

She considered his story. "Is that why you only work cold cases at Finding the Lost? Like my sister's case? Like Molly's?" Jordan had been a key player in finding little Molly James, Erica's daughter, who'd been kidnapped three years ago. Molly had been reunited with her mother six months before and was adjusting well thanks to a team effort. That was one case Katie would never forget. She'd worked countless hours looking for Molly and had forged a deep friendship with Erica as a result.

Jordan's nostrils flared, her insight seeming to surprise him. "It's that obvious, huh?"

She shrugged. "Maybe not to the ordinary person, but I just put two and two together."

"Right." Jordan tossed his napkin onto the table like he'd lost his appetite. "Can we get into the details about your sister's case?"

She'd pushed enough. "I suppose it's time."

Jordan steepled his fingers and said, "Two weeks ago, you asked us to look into your sister's disappearance."

"Right."

She shook her head. "I can't believe it's already been fourteen years. In some ways it seems like she's been gone forever. In others, it seems like it was yesterday."

"I took the information you gave me and the information from the file and tried to piece together the events of that day. I wanted to bounce everything off of you, see if you had anything else to add." He paused. "And would have already done so if you had taken my calls."

She grimaced. He stayed silent, but kept his gaze on her face. "I'm sorry. It's not your fault." Katie paused and considered what she wanted to tell him. She finally said, "You know, I became a detective because of Lucy."

He nodded. "Erica mentioned something along those lines."

"In the beginning, I did what I could on my own time to find her. But I kept running into brick walls. I got frustrated and angry that I wasn't making any progress. It became an . . . obsession. Once again, the case was taking over my life." She licked her lips and took a swig of her iced tea. "The first time was when she was taken. My parents worked so hard to find her — flyers, press conferences, interviews, everything. And of course I did what I could to be involved and help, but I was fourteen. I was powerless." She swallowed hard.

"I hated that feeling. But now *I* was doing something." She sighed. "My lieutenant had been very understanding, but I'd reached the limit on his patience. He was ready to put me on suspension because I was letting it affect my performance on my other cases. I had to stop if I wanted to save my career, my sanity. So I did."

And she felt guilty for that. "I told myself I would take a break and get back to it. And I came to Finding the Lost because I thought it would be good to have some outside help to keep me from becoming obsessed."

"How long has your break been?"

"A year."

"So after a year, you decide to start searching again. Why the hesitation now?"

She rubbed her eyes. "Part of me is scared that I'll do it again. Let it become an obsession. And as much as I want to know what happened to her, that can't happen. And —" she picked at imaginary lint on the sleeve of her fleece "— I'm afraid of what I'm — we're — going to find."

"You're scared we're going to find out she's dead."

Katie looked up. "It's been fourteen years, Jordan. You know the odds as well as I do." She took a deep breath. "Don't get me wrong. I want to know what happened to her. And yet . . . I don't."

"You can't have it both ways." He gentled his tone.

"I know that." She rubbed a hand down her weary face and closed her eyes. "I just . . . What if she's dead?" she whispered. "How will I tell my parents that? How will I live with it?"

Jordan leaned over and took her hand. The warmth of his fingers on hers made her shiver. "Won't it give you some closure? One way or the other? All these years you've held out hope. Even if she's dead, wouldn't you finally be able to put it behind you?"

Katie shrugged and bit her lip then said, "I don't know. That's the problem. I simply don't know."

Jordan sighed. "Well, I've got information. I need to know what you want me to do with it."

She shook her head. "Finding Lucy is why I'm here. I've been kidding myself thinking I could just let it go permanently." She took a deep breath and met his gaze. "I've got to know one way or another — and I think my parents do, too." After shredding her napkin into tiny pieces, she firmed her lips and looked him in the eye. "So tell me."

Jordan pulled at his lower lip. Then he said, "I called a friend at the bureau and asked him about the case, got the file emailed to me and did some research. Your lieutenant was nice enough to let me have the local law enforcement file so I could compare the two." He set that on the table in front of her.

She glanced at it. "Who have you talked to so far?"

"A lot of people. Particularly those who still live in your old neighborhood."

"Go on."

He pulled out a notebook and flipped through a few pages. "I tried to get in touch with your neighbor Elaine Johnson."

"She's still alive?" Katie asked.

It surprised him she didn't know. "Yes. She's old, but she's definitely alive. The only problem is, she wasn't home. I've been by her house three times and she's not there. I asked some of your neighbors where she is and one of them thought she was visiting her son in Georgia. Another said she was in the hospital. And yet another said she thought she was in a nursing home. I'm tracking her down."

"How about that. Elaine Johnson's still alive." She gave a breathy laugh. "Wow. I mean, I knew she was a year ago, but she was in the hospital with congestive heart failure the last I heard. I ended up deciding to take my break before I was able to talk to her, but I would scan the obituaries in the paper thinking I'd see her name. When I never did, I figured I just missed it." She bit her lip and shook her head. "She didn't see anything anyway that day. She was with me in the house when it all happened."

Jordan nodded. Elaine Johnson. The next-door neighbor who'd needed help with her groceries. Katie had carried several bags into the house and then returned to her front yard to find Lucy missing.

She swallowed hard. "Who else have you had a chance to talk to?"

"Some of the other neighbors, but no one seemed to notice anything odd that day — until you called the cops and they swarmed the neighborhood. I'm still trying to track down a few people I haven't gotten in touch with, people who've moved out of the neighborhood, but there aren't many. I want to question every neighbor who was within sight of your old front yard."

"I already did that, but maybe a new person asking even the same questions will spark something that'll produce different answers." One could hope. "A couple of hours after Lucy disappeared, I remember the detective, Frank Miller, coming out and questioning everyone even though the uniformed officers had already done it." She finished off her last slice of pizza. "I watched him go house to house. I even followed him to see if I could listen in and learn anything."

"Did you?"

"No. In fact, he was mad when he caught me. Told me to go on home and let him do his job. I remember smarting off to him and telling him he must not be much of a detective since my sister was still missing." Jordan winced and she nodded. "Yeah, he wasn't too happy with that."

"I guess not."

"I still see him around the precinct every once in a while. He goes out of his way to avoid me."

"Detective Frank Miller. I spoke to him, too. He feels bad about not finding Lucy.

It's obvious that talking about the case brings back unpleasant memories, a sense of failure." Jordan flipped the page in his notebook. "He's forty-five years old now. Your sister's case was one of his first, but his partner, Danny Jackson, was a veteran."

"I talked to him last year, too. He retired a few years ago."

"He was close to retirement fourteen years ago. He said your sister's is one of the cases that still haunts him."

"So did talking to them help? Because it didn't do much for me. He's very gruff, but I don't think I should take it personally. I think it's just how he is."

"He was gruff with me, too. And I'm not sure if talking to him helped. He basically told me to mind my own business. I'm still going through the file and all their notes." He tapped the notebook against his palm and studied the woman across from him.

She intrigued him and while he didn't want it to be so, it was. For the first time in a long time, he was attracted to someone. Interested in getting to know her on a deeper level than just a working relationship.

And it had to be someone he couldn't pursue. He pictured his parents' reaction if he were to announce that he was seeing the woman they blamed for their younger son's death.

And winced.

No, unfortunately, Katie Randall was off-limits.

Her phone rang and she snagged it. "Hello?"

"Ms. Randall, this is Deep Clean Services. I just wanted to let you know we arrived at your house about seven-thirty this morning and will be done in about an hour."

"Thanks for letting me know."

She made payment arrangements, hung up and told Jordan the news. "Guess that means Mariah and I can go home." She frowned. "Strangely enough, I'm mourning the Christmas tree the most." Katie sent a text to her roommate to let her know, then turned back to the file. "All right. What else is in here?"

Katie moved over to sit beside Jordan in the booth so they could see the file without one of them having to try and read upside down.

Sitting beside him, she noticed his cologne once again, the strength that emanated from him. His warmth. She shivered at being so near him and swallowed hard. An attraction to this man was just not an option. And yet no matter how much her mind protested, her heart had decided to take matters into its own hands.

Focus. *Focus.* "You know I got this file from the department and copied everything in it. I used to study it at night when I couldn't sleep." Which had been often.

They scanned the notes, turning the pages one by one. A small slip of paper, stuck to the back of the sheet she'd just been reading, caught the edge of her fingernail and fell off. Katie picked it up. "What's this?"

Jordan took it from her. "Looks like an address."

"It was stuck to the back of this. Looks like there's food or something on it." She scraped the mess off with her fingernail. "How did I miss this?" she muttered. She knew how. She'd been in a hurry to get the file copied before her boss caught her once again working her sister's case and had returned the original file without seeing the small slip of paper. "Let's see where the address is." She grabbed her phone and punched it in the GPS app. She looked up at him. "It's a place called Jake's Diner. About thirty miles away, in Anderson." Katie bit her lip. "Why would this be in here?"

"It's a sticky note. Probably Frank or Danny answered the phone and wrote it down. Is there anything else with that information on it?" he asked.

They flipped through the file again. Twice. Katie shook her head. "Nothing."

Jordan rubbed his chin. "Feel like a road trip?"

She stood. "Definitely. Let's go." Katie headed for the cash register and Jordan followed.

At the door, he said, "I'll get the car. You pay."

She gaped at him. He widened his eyes, the picture of innocence. "What? I wouldn't want you to think I was trying to turn this into a date or anything."

Katie felt the flush start at the base of her throat. "Cute, Gray. Real cute."

He winked. "I'll get the next one."

FOUR

Jordan gave himself a mental smack upside the head as he pulled his car around. Mere minutes ago, he'd reminded himself that an attraction to Katie was not a good thing, and then he'd turned around and deliberately flirted with her. What was he thinking? He sure didn't want to give her the wrong idea.

Or the right idea. That he was interested in her. Because that interest could go nowhere as long as his parents blamed her for Neil's death. He groaned and rubbed his eyes. *Lord, I'm going to need Your guidance on this one.*

He could see Katie inside paying. His phone rang and when he saw his father's number on the screen, guilt swamped him. Swallowing it back, he hit the talk button. "Hi, Dad."

"You busy, son?"

"Working a case, but I've got a couple of

minutes. What's up?"

"You mother wanted me to call and invite you to dinner Sunday night. Can you make it?"

Jordan ran through his schedule in his head as Katie walked toward him. She climbed in, and he said, "I can make it."

"Great. Around five-thirty?"

"Sure, Dad. I'll be there."

Katie buckled her seat belt and checked her phone.

Jordan hung up. Katie looked at him. "Your dad?"

"Yeah."

She nodded.

"What are your parents like?" he asked. She blinked and a deep sorrow crossed her face. Then she smiled. A smile so forced it nearly broke his heart.

She sighed. "They're good people. I get along better with my father than my mother." The smile slid off. "Ever since Lucy's disappearance, she's battled depression, has trouble getting out of bed most days." She shrugged and looked out the window. "People in their church have tried to reach out and help, but she doesn't respond much."

"I'm sorry." Jordan cranked the car and made a mental note not to go there again.

"Thanks. I am, too." She looked back at him and he could make out anger mixed with the sorrow. Then she lowered her gaze. "Is it wrong that I get really angry with her sometimes?"

Her voice was so low he had to strain to make out the words. "No. I can imagine fourteen years of depression would be very tiring."

"It's not just that. I don't even know that she can help it, but I needed her, too —" She flushed and shook her head. "Never mind." She took a deep breath and cleared her throat. "Speaking of my mother —" She pulled her phone from her pocket and dialed a number. "Hi, Mom." Jordan heard the woman's muffled answer, then Katie said, "Your dinner is being delivered. They're coming around five-thirty, all right?" She listened a moment. "No, Mom, you won't have to worry about washing or returning any pans. They'll all be disposable, okay? I hope you enjoy it."

More indistinguishable words and then a sigh from Katie as she said goodbye and hung up.

He couldn't help it. "What was that about?"

"Dad called me the day before yesterday and said my mom had a doctor's appointment today. My partner's sister, Christi, has a catering business. I asked her to deliver dinner to my parents tonight so they wouldn't have to worry about it. In all the excitement, I forgot to let them know."

"That's really thoughtful." Jordan eyed her.

She shrugged and flushed. "I don't know if thoughtful is the right —" She bit the words off and nearly chewed a hole in her lower lip.

"What?"

"Never mind. It's not important."

But it was, he could tell. However, he dropped the subject as he turned in to the parking lot of Jake's Diner. Dropped it, but didn't forget it. The woman intrigued him, and he wanted to know what it was she hadn't said. But that would wait.

They climbed from the vehicle, tugging their coats tighter against the wind. Katie walked at a fast clip toward the door and Jordan followed her.

The diner looked like a throwback to the fifties. A well-preserved throwback. With her hand on the door handle, Katie said, "Nice."

"Yeah. How come I didn't know about this place?"

She shrugged. "I've heard it mentioned in conversation, but never bothered to drive out here. I'll have to make sure I do that sometime soon. Just for fun."

"Maybe I'll come with you." He gave her a slow smile and she flushed.

Then lifted her chin. "Maybe I'll let you."

Cars zipped past on the highway. Several slowed and turned in.

One slowed almost to a stop in the middle of the road, catching Jordan's attention. "Look."

Katie looked. The car sped up and was soon gone from sight. She frowned. "What do you think that was all about?"

"I have no idea, but I've got the make and model."

They entered the diner and walked up to the bar area. Multicolored lights hung above and blinked in time with the Christmas carol coming from the speaker to her right.

Katie slid onto one of the silver, red-cushioned stools and Jordan sat beside her. For a few minutes, they watched the waitress scurry about taking orders, her red-and-white hat tipped with a bell that jingled at every shake of her head. Now she stood in front of Katie. "What'll it be?"

"I'll have a coffee."

Jordan said, "Same here."

Katie pulled out the picture of her sister that had been splashed all over the news when she'd disappeared fourteen years ago. When the waitress came back with their coffee, Katie eyed her name tag and asked, "Celia, how long have you been working here?"

Celia tilted her head and lifted a hand to hold the hat in place. She snapped her gum and said, "About six years now, I guess."

"Is there anyone that's been here for at least fourteen or fifteen years?"

"The owner. Been here twenty-seven years, as she likes to remind us on a regular basis."

"Who's the owner?"

"Betty June Clark."

"Is she here?"

"Somewhere." Her gaze darted to the newcomers walking in.

Katie flashed her badge. "You mind telling her we'd like to ask her a couple of questions?"

Now she had Celia's full attention. With wide eyes, she backed toward the kitchen. "Hey, Betty! You got company out here."

"Thanks," Katie said and sipped her coffee. Jordan dumped three things of flavored creamer into his. Katie nearly choked when he took the silver-topped sugar jar and dumped at least the equivalent of ten tablespoons into the steaming brew. "You like a little coffee with your cream and sugar, huh?"

He grinned and took a sip. "Yep."

In the mirror on the opposite wall, Katie watched the crowd behind her. She normally liked to sit with her back to the wall, but the place was packed and with the mirror she felt a little less like a target.

A woman in a black skirt, navy blue button-down shirt and white tennis shoes came from the kitchen. She eyed Jordan and Katie with wary curiosity. "Can I help you?"

Katie introduced herself and Jordan and studied the pretty woman. "You don't look old enough to have been here twenty-seven years."

Betty's tension lightened. She smiled. "Started working here when I was sixteen. I'm forty-three now. Took over when my daddy retired seventeen years ago."

Jordan asked, "Do you remember a local kidnapping case fourteen years ago? Lucy Randall?"

Betty stilled and her brow furrowed, eyes narrowed. "I remember. Very well, actually. Was all over the news for weeks."

"That's the one."

Betty nodded. "My baby sister was the same age as Lucy when it happened. That kidnapping has haunted me and my family for more reasons than one."

Katie perked up as her blood started to hum in anticipation. "Why's that?"

"Because I believe Lucy and her kidnapper stopped here to eat."

Katie jerked and felt the blood drain from her face. That would be a good enough reason for the woman to recall the details so clearly. "Why do you say that?"

"The guy had on a baseball cap and sunglasses and didn't take them off the whole time they were in here. The little girl's hair was whacked off like it had been done in a hurry without any care for style. When I cleaned the bathrooms, I saw a few strands of hair that looked like the same color as hers around the toilet in the men's bathroom. Our floor is dark wood. That hair stood out. And besides, that little girl just wasn't acting right."

"How was she acting?"

"She was jumpy and scared. At least that's what I thought."

"What color was her hair?" If it stood out against a dark floor, Katie had a good idea what the answer was.

"Blond. That fine white blond that comes naturally to the lucky few."

Katie swallowed hard. Lucy had had that kind of hair. Katie's hair was blond, too, but not like Lucy's. Lucy's had been so blond it had almost been white.

"Why didn't you call the police?" Katie forced the words past the lump in her throat.

"I did."

"You did?" Katie stared.

Jordan jumped in. "What happened?"

"They came out here, and I told them the same thing I told you."

"Did they get a crime scene unit over here?" Katie asked. She hadn't seen anything in the file to indicate one had checked the place out. At the very least, they should have gotten a sample of hair to compare to something of Lucy's — like a piece of hair from her hairbrush.

At the very least.

"No. It was just a couple of detectives who came out and asked a few questions. One looked at the bathroom, the other talked to me for a few minutes. When the one in the bathroom came out, he just said he'd be in touch if he had any more questions."

Katie drew in a deep breath and exchanged an incredulous look with Jordan. "Unbelievable," he muttered. His napkin fluttered to the floor. He and Katie bent at the same time to retrieve it.

A crack sounded. Betty screamed as the sugar jar in front of Jordan exploded.

Jordan spun, grabbed his weapon even as he ducked for cover. From the corner of his eye, he noticed Katie doing the same. Another blast came from outside the diner and hit the mirror over the bar. Katie screamed, "Get down! Get down! Call nine-one-one!"

The deafening chaos surrounding him, Jordan hit the floor, then scrambled to one of the unoccupied booths. Betty yelled into her cell phone as she crouched behind the bar.

A squeal of tires, a burst of horns and one sickening crunch followed by two more sent Jordan racing for the door of the diner. Katie followed. Outside, he saw the wreckage on the busy road. Katie turned to the patrons and hollered, "Everyone stay back and stay away from the windows!"

"You see him?" Jordan asked, scanning the area even as he moved toward the pileup. A car peeled away.

"There he goes!" Katie yelled.

"He'll just have to go," Jordan said between clenched teeth. "We've got to make sure no one's hurt. Come on." He got on the phone and called in the direction the shooter was heading.

A woman stumbled from the three-car wreck, holding her bleeding head. "He stole my car!" Katie bolted over. She gripped the young woman by her upper arms and led her away from the vehicles. "He had a gun and he hit me with it."

The woman's tears flowed while Jordan called back to let them know the vehicle was stolen. "I need CSU here, too."

Kate settled the distraught woman on the curb. She looked to be in her early twenties. Petite and soft. Defenseless. An easy target. "What's your name?" Katie asked.

"Miranda."

"Did you get a good look at him, Miranda?"

"No. He came from behind and pulled me out. I never saw his face. But he had a rifle strapped to his back and a pistol in his right hand. I saw those real clear."

"Stay here."

Sirens sounded in the distance. Jordan left Katie with Miranda and went to see who else needed help. He asked a young woman with a toddler strapped into a car seat in the back of her minivan, "Are you all right? Your child?"

Oh, Lord, please, not a child.

But the woman nodded as she unbuckled

the crying little one, her scared, pinched features doubling his determination to catch the person who'd caused this.

An older gentleman in a gray Taurus held his neck. Jordan jogged over to him. "Sir? Don't move, help's on the way."

"I'm all right. Did you see that idiot? Pulled right out of the parking lot and wrecked his car, then stole another one."

"You saw him?"

"Clear as day."

"What's your name?"

"Bobby Young."

"We'll get you checked out and then I'll need to get a statement from you, all right? We'll want you to meet with a sketch artist, too."

"Sure, sure. Whatever I can do to help catch that maniac."

Four police cruisers pulled into the area, blue lights flashing. Two officers made their way to him, and Jordan flashed his badge then gave them a rundown on what he'd done.

"We'll take it from here. Thanks."

Three ambulances arrived, and the paramedics got to work.

Jordan found Katie taking statements and keeping people clear of the wreck. She glanced at him. "CSU on the way?"

"Yes, along with everyone else."

Three fire trucks screamed onto the scene. Katie nodded. "Good."

Jordan knew he might be overstepping his bounds. Technically, while he was employed with the FBI, the FBI didn't handle car wrecks or local shootings, but he figured since one of those bullets came mighty close to having his name on it, he'd just work as though he belonged there. At least until someone told him otherwise.

Katie grabbed his arm to get his attention in all the chaos. She held up her phone. "Just got a call. He got away. They can't find any sign of him anywhere."

Jordan nodded. He wasn't surprised.

The crime scene unit van pulled into the diner parking lot. Jordan followed Katie and waited as the vehicle parked on the edge of the lot.

Katie watched Faith Nelson climb from the van. "I'm glad you're here."

"What happened?"

Katie filled her in as the woman grabbed her gear from the back of the van. To help process the scene, Faith had brought three of her team. Two headed for the diner; Faith and her other coworker started in the parking lot. "Where was he parked?"

"I'm not sure." She pointed to the street where Jordan directed traffic around the crunched vehicles. "But he ended up in that wreck before he stole another car that wasn't involved in the accident."

Faith delegated assignments to her team and headed over to the shooter's vehicle. Katie followed. Jordan tucked his phone in his pocket and looked at her. "The car's stolen."

"Naturally."

Faith shrugged. "I'll do the best I can do here. Will be able to do more once we get it to the lab." She glanced at Katie. "I'll have Mariah work on it."

Katie nodded. "Thanks."

The crime scene photographer had his work cut out for him between the wreck and the diner. She noticed he had someone with him to help. For the next two hours, Katie worked the scene and listened as Jordan offered his opinion and expertise. He kept a low profile and didn't try to take over, although he might have wanted to. That bullet had come awfully close to his head. If she hadn't dropped her napkin —

"You ready to get out of here?"

Jordan's low voice cut into her thoughts.

"I'm ready."

Katie looked back at where the wreck had

been. Broken bits of glass that had escaped the sweep-up were the only sign of the chaos from just a few hours earlier. The diner was another matter — crime scene tape and broken windows were evidence of the reality of what had happened.

She climbed into Jordan's truck and put on her seat belt. He said, "The car that the shooter was driving was the one that slowed down right before we went in the diner."

"You sure?"

"Pretty sure. Same color, make and model. A red Toyota Camry."

"So you think he followed us, let us go in and then came back to shoot the place up?"

"Yes."

She mentally chewed on that for a minute. "If you hadn't ducked, that bullet would have hit you in the back of the head."

He grimaced and reached up to rub the back of his neck, as though he needed reassurance it was still in one piece. "We're making someone uncomfortable. Someone who knows we're investigating your sister's kidnapping."

For the first time in a long time, hope sprouted. "If we're making someone uncomfortable in regards to Lucy's kidnapping, we must be onto something."

"I think that diner was a huge clue."

"So why wasn't it in the report?"

"That's a question for Detective Miller." He gave her a grim smile. "Plus we have an eyewitness. Bobby Young said he saw the man clear as day."

"Is he on his way to the precinct to work with the sketch artist?"

"He is."

Katie pulled out her phone and dialed the number she hadn't used in a year. He answered on the third ring. "Miller here."

"Hi, Frank. It's Katie Randall." Silence greeted her. "Lucy Randall's sister."

"I know who you are. What can I do for you?"

"I was wondering if you'd have some time to discuss my sister's case with me."

He grunted. "You're back on that, are you?"

She didn't let his gruffness deter her. "I am."

"You working with that guy from Finding the Lost?"

"Yes."

He huffed a sigh. "All right. Sure. I don't know what else you think I can tell you that I didn't tell him, but how about four o'clock tomorrow afternoon here at the station?"

"I'll be there."

She hung up and filled Jordan in. "Do you

70

mind if I come along?" he asked.

"Not at all."

"I wonder what he'll have to say about the diner."

"Good question. But until then, I'm curious to see if Mr. Wray has anything to add to his story about why he was in my house."

"Shall we find out?"

She glanced at her watch. "Let's see if we can catch him before he heads to dinner."

Jordan followed Katie into the jail. The usual chaos — ringing phones, chattering of law enforcement and curses from recently arrested criminals — filled the air. It reminded him of his detective days before he'd applied to the FBI and gotten the case that had turned his life upside down.

But he wasn't here to think about that. Right now he wanted to know if Mr. Wray had anything else to add to his story.

Katie had called ahead and asked for him to be brought into one of the private areas where prisoners met with those involved in their legal activities. Katie paced the length of the small room while Jordan leaned against the table.

She said, "I wonder if he's retained a lawyer yet."

"Probably a public defender. I looked a

little deeper into his past last night. He was on probation. His latest crime will land him here for a good long while."

"Then maybe he won't have anything to lose by talking to us now."

"Maybe."

She shot him a glance and then looked at her watch. "Wonder what's taking so long?"

"He's probably at dinner."

She grimaced. "Is it already that time? I forgot how late it was."

"Your headache gone?"

"The one from this morning is. However, I have a feeling Mr. Wray may spark another one."

The door opened and Jordan straightened.

An officer said, "Mr. Wray won't be coming in."

"Why's that?" Katie asked.

"Because he's being transported to the hospital. There was a fight on the way to the dining hall. He was stabbed in the throat."

FIVE

Katie pushed the rotating door of the hospital and stepped into the emergency department waiting room. She flashed her badge to the woman behind the desk. "Wesley Wray. He was just brought in from the prison. Stabbing victim."

The woman got on the phone. She looked up. "I'm sorry. He died in the ambulance."

Katie let out a breath she hadn't realized she'd been holding. She nodded. "All right. Thanks." She looked at Jordan. "Great. Just great."

"Yeah." He placed a hand on her lower back as he directed her to the door. Now that her adrenaline rush was ebbing, disappointment flooded her. As did her awareness of the man beside her. Their moments together flashed in her mind. He'd been nothing but kind and considerate with her, thoughtful and selfless. Spending time with him was giving her a new perspective of him and she liked it.

"What are you plans tomorrow?" he asked.

"Thursday. I plan to have breakfast with my parents and then work late. You?"

He gave her an amused look. "Something along those lines. I probably won't see my parents, but I'll definitely be working late."

"Do you see your parents often?"

He paused. "Most Saturdays. You?"

"Most Thursday mornings."

He opened the car door for her and she lifted a brow in surprise. He shrugged. "Chivalry's not dead, in spite of what most people think."

She smiled. "I like chivalry." She slipped into the passenger seat and buckled up. When he settled behind the wheel, she said, "Probably because I don't get much of it."

"Because you're a cop or because you just pick the wrong guys?"

She shot him a perturbed look. "Partly because I'm a cop, I suppose. I've chosen what was once a male-only field. My feminine side gets ignored mostly."

He turned the key and pulled from the parking lot. "Does that bother you?"

She hesitated. "Only sometimes. Depends on the circumstances."

"Like?"

"If I'm on a date and it gets ignored, yes,

it bothers me. Working a case with a fellow officer, I don't even think about it."

"Do you go on dates often?" he asked.

His casual tone gave no hint as to the purpose behind the question. Was he asking because he was just curious or was there something more? Like personal interest.

"No. I haven't been on a date since my fiancé died a few years ago." As soon as the words left her lips, she wanted to recall them.

He stiffened and shot her a brief look. "What happened?"

"He was shot. He was a detective and walked into the wrong building at the wrong time. He and his partner were set up and ambushed. They never had a chance." She kept her words short, hoping Jordan would back off the line of questioning she'd opened up. "So, are you ready to call it a night?"

He didn't say anything and she wondered if he'd let her change the subject. The he said, "Who do you think killed Wray?"

"Someone who didn't want him talking to us."

"Which means Wray didn't pick my house randomly. He had a purpose in being there and I want to know what it was."

Jordan said, "It seems like he was looking

for something."

"Like my laptop," she mused. "Remember? He asked if it was in my case."

"So what's on the laptop that would be of interest to someone?"

"Nothing. I don't keep work stuff on there, just personal stuff, mostly."

"And notes about Lucy's kidnapping?"

She stilled then nodded. "Yes. There are notes about Lucy on there."

"Interesting."

"Isn't it, though?" She sighed. "Are you ready to call it a night?"

"Yes, I guess I am. What time are you available tomorrow?"

"I'll be done by midmorning. I'm just running a few errands for my mother."

"All right. You like Chinese food?"

"Love it."

"Where do you want to meet?"

"Why don't you come to my house?" She held up Lucy's paper file. "I think I have this thing memorized, but I'm going to work on it tonight. I'm also going to check in with Mariah and see if she got anything from the diner."

"Will you let me know what you find out?"

"Of course."

Jordan dropped her at her car and Katie watched him drive away, wondering at the ball of tension in the pit of her stomach.

As she drove home, she couldn't get her mind off the handsome FBI agent. Why had she mentioned her fiancé? As a way of letting Jordan know she was single? He already knew that. A way of telling him she was ready to move on?

Was she? Maybe. But not with him. At least not while his parents still held so much animosity toward her. So what had mentioning her fiancé been all about?

Headlights in her rearview mirror captured her attention. The driver had them on bright and kept creeping closer. Katie adjusted the mirror and alternated keeping her eye on the lights behind her and the road before her.

Her phone rang, and she snatched it from the cup holder. "Hello?"

"Hey." Mariah's soft alto came over the line. "I've been working on the evidence the team gathered from that shooting at the diner."

"And?"

"The car had tons of fingerprints. Lots of little ones belonging to children that I can probably rule out. The others will take time to go through."

"Well, it was stolen, so that's to be expected."

"Right, it was reported stolen three days ago, but I did find a receipt for gas you might want to check out. Someone filled up early this morning."

"Cash or credit?"

"Cash."

"Naturally." She chewed her lip and glanced at the lights in the mirror again. Still on bright and so close they helped illuminate the road in front of her. "All right, text me the address. Maybe they've got some video I can look at."

Mariah said, "Done."

The phone beeped, confirming Mariah's text.

"When are you coming home? I'm on my way there now."

"I'm not. I'm going back over to Grandma Jean's. She's come down with a nasty virus, so I told her I'd stay with her at night. My mom's there now."

"Uh-oh. I'm sorry."

"Yeah. Just pray I don't catch it."

"You're never sick."

"True," Mariah said happily. "I've got to go. I'll call if I come up with anything else."

Katie hung up and took one more look in her rearview mirror. Enough was enough. Checking around her, she turned her signal on and pulled over to the side. She muttered, "Go on, then, if you're so impatient. But if you speed, you're mine."

But the car pulled up behind her.

Okay, so this wasn't about someone in a hurry.

She looked around. Darkness coated the area. Uneasiness crawled up her spine as she debated what she was going to do. Crawl out of the car and confront him? Wait for him to approach her?

But he was just sitting there and she couldn't see enough to figure out who he might be.

True, she was a cop and she had her weapon, but no way was she going to be caught alone on a relatively empty road after dark with someone intent on playing a dangerous game. She gunned the engine, grabbed her phone and dialed Gregory's number.

No answer.

She hung up and punched in Jordan's. The car followed her into the street, rammed his gas and bumped her. Hard. Katie jerked against the seat belt and lost her grip on the phone. It tumbled to the floorboard. She left it there and grasped the wheel to control the vehicle.

Katie gripped the wheel and put some of her defensive-driving skills to work. She slammed on the brakes and spun the wheel to the left. The tailgating vehicle roared past. Cars approached from behind. Her possible assailant took off. Katie gripped the wheel to go after the disappearing taillights, but by the time she got back on the road and headed after him, he'd vanished.

She slapped the wheel in frustration. She didn't even have a tag to call in.

Katie pulled to the side of the road once again and reached down to feel for her phone. She grasped it and noticed Jordan had called her five times. She hit redial.

"Are you all right?" he shouted.

"I'm fine." She relayed the car incident. "He's gone and I'm going home."

"Are you sure you're okay?"

"Yes. But I'll be sleeping with my gun tonight."

Jordan paced his den, knowing he was going to wear a groove in the floor if he didn't sit down. But he couldn't. His nerves hummed and his adrenaline still flowed from the excitement with Katie.

"You okay?"

He spun to see his roommate, Brandon Hayes, standing in the door. "Yeah. I'm okay. Had a scary moment a few minutes ago, but it's all good now." When his phone rang with Katie's number popping up on the screen, he'd had a leap of gladness, a thrill he hadn't felt in a long time.

When he'd heard nothing but the squeal of tires, Katie's yell and then silence as the phone went dead, his elation had quickly turned to fear. He'd been halfway to his car, with no idea of where he was going or how he was going to find her, when she'd finally called him back.

"What happened?"

Jordan filled him in.

"Whoa. But she's all right?"

"Yeah. At least she says she is."

"Can I help with anything?"

Jordan paced the length of his den, debating whether or not to go over to her house. But she'd sounded fine. A little shaken maybe, but unhurt. Indecision made him hesitate.

"No. I guess not."

"Let me know if you need something."

An idea occurred to him. "If I need help with some surveillance, would you have some time?"

Brandon nodded. "Just not tonight. I'm already doing some for a case."

"Great. Thanks."

Jordan's phone rang, and Brandon walked back down the hall toward his bedroom.

Jordan glanced at the phone display. His new boss with the FBI, Special Agent in Charge Ruby Parker. "What can I do for you, ma'am?"

"I need you to look into something for me."

"What's that?"

She hesitated. "It's a predator and a missing kid."

"No."

"Excuse me?"

"Look, the FBI asked me to be available for some contract work. I agreed, but one of the conditions was no missing children."

She huffed. "I don't understand you, Jordan. You work for an organization that finds missing children. I need you on this one." Her frustration came through loud and clear.

"I handle the adult cases only. Or children's cold cases. Cases where the victim's probably already dead and the family just wants closure. I don't do anything else. That was the agreement with Finding the Lost. That's the agreement with the FBI. Nothing's changed."

"Then I don't see that we need to keep you on."

"Look —"

"I'll be in touch."

She hung up, and Jordan slowly lowered the phone, visions of his past coming back to haunt him. Missing children. He simply couldn't do missing kids. Not anymore. Not since he'd let little Regina Palmer die. Even though no one blamed him for the child's death, Jordan couldn't seem to find a way to get past the guilt.

He drew in a ragged breath.

He wasn't worried about Ruby getting rid of him. She knew the deal.

And right now he wanted to focus on helping Katie. His gut told him they'd asked the right questions of the right person. Only he wasn't sure which questions had sparked the panic in whoever seemed to be targeting Katie.

Which meant they could narrow the list. Sort of. He'd already talked to over forty people.

He wondered how Mr. Young had done with the sketch artist and made a mental note to ask Katie about it first thing.

Jordan glanced at the clock once again. Seven o'clock. She should be home by now. Without waiting to talk himself out of it, he grabbed his phone and texted her.

You all right?

Within seconds, her reply buzzed him.

I'm home and going over the file. Trying to figure out who we've made nervous.

He chuckled.

Great minds think alike.

LOL. You, too?

Yes. Any news from the sketch artist?

No. And that's weird. I'll give her a call.

Let me know what she says. See you tomorrow.

Nite.

Jordan set the phone aside, feeling a little better now that he knew she was safe in her home. Still . . .

Brandon reentered the room, dressed in a heavy coat, gloves and a warm cap. He had a scarf thrown over his left shoulder. "I'll be gone until morning."

"How does it feel to be a full-time detective again?"

"Feels good. I needed to take the time off

to help Erica with Finding the Lost, and I'll always be available, but being back on the job feels like I can breathe again, you know?"

He knew. Once a cop, always a cop. Exactly how he felt about being back on the FBI payroll.

"Be careful."

"Always."

Brandon left. Jordan grabbed his phone again and hit a number he had on speed dial.

Katie checked the locks on her doors and windows one more time, then settled on the couch with the file she nearly had memorized. Only this time she had new material to work with.

Jordan's notes.

She flipped the pages and studied the tight, neat words. Names of her parents' neighbors leaped out at her. One after the other. She finished Jordan's notes then started again. She'd talked to everyone he had — and they all said the same thing.

With one exception: the McKinneys. Her heart picked up a little speed.

The McKinneys had been in their early thirties when Lucy disappeared.

Mr. McKinney had been in a car wreck

the week before. Mrs. McKinney had brought him home about three hours before the kidnapping, but stated she hadn't heard or seen anything out of the ordinary. However, she'd wanted to know if anyone had looked into the car she'd seen several days in a row, parked down the street from the Randall household. Mrs. McKinney thought it strange that she never saw it again after the kidnapping.

Katie's heart picked up speed.

Jordan had noted it was a gray sedan. A Buick, possibly, but Mrs. McKinney just wasn't sure of the make and model.

Katie pondered the idea that the car might mean something. Might somehow be an important piece of information. Could be. Then again, it could have belonged to someone on the street. Someone who had family visiting. Could have been a rental. Could have been anything.

Or it could have been the kidnapper staking out the area.

She reached for her phone to call Mrs. McKinney then looked at the time again. She blinked. Four hours had passed since she'd sat down with the file. Reading and rereading.

Exhaustion swamped her, only slightly lessening the excitement she felt at a possible new lead. Katie rubbed her eyes and set the file aside.

She needed sleep. Mrs. McKinney could wait until tomorrow. She checked the doors again, peered through the windows and checked her weapon one more time.

Was she safe?

Probably not, but she'd done everything in her power to give herself a fighting chance should she need it.

Jordan woke from a nightmare. One he'd had since the little girl had died on his watch. She kept calling for him to save her and he couldn't. Sweat coated him and he knew he wouldn't sleep again for a while. Katie instantly came to mind. He picked up his phone and dialed his buddy Cortland Buchanan, a retired FBI agent who'd settled in the area. He'd agreed to keep an eye on Katie's house tonight.

"Hey, Cort. Any activity going on over there?" he asked.

"Not a thing. Quiet and uneventful."

"Good."

"What are you doing up? Another nightmare?"

"Yeah." Only Brandon and Cortland knew about the nightmares.

"Sorry."

"I know."

"I'll let you know if anything happens."

"You staying awake all right?"

"I am. Coffee is my friend."

"And a few doughnuts?"

"I hate to admit to being a stereotype, but . . ."

Jordan felt the nightmare leaving him, felt his muscles relax their death grip and ease into a less painful state. "All right, buddy, call if you need me. I'll be up awhile."

"Drink some hot tea. Decaf. Does wonders for me."

Jordan grimaced. "Right." Not likely.

He hung up and grabbed his remote. Then tossed it on the bed. Why make Cort lose any more sleep when Jordan wasn't going to be closing his eyes any time soon?

He picked up the phone again.

Katie choked and sat upright in her bed, blinking the sleep from her eyes. And still her vision was hazy. What had awakened her? Her ears rang and she shook her head. Only to realize the screech wasn't inside her mind, but coming from the house.

Her fire alarm. Awareness shot through her. She stumbled from under the covers and knocked the lamp over. The crash resounded as smoke continued to fill the air. Katie groped for the light switch in her closet. Flames shot up around the bedroom door she'd closed and locked as an extra measure of protection.

She grabbed her cell phone from the bedside table and punched in 911. She raced to the window and stopped to stare. A hole in her glass pane in the shape of a perfect circle stunned her. She blinked and realized she wasn't seeing things. Someone had cut the glass.

Mariah! Relief crashed through her as she remembered Mariah had stayed with her grandmother again.

"Nine-one-one, what's your emergency?"

"My house is on fire," she gasped.

"What's your address?"

Katie told her. She glanced back at the spreading flames and thought she saw an object, but she wasn't sure. The flames grew as though on steroids, biting, grabbing at everything in their path. Soon it would be her.

But she had to know. Katie dropped to the floor where she was able to grab some air. She moved toward the flames until the heat became unbearable. She gasped, choked on the lungful of smoke and scrambled back, but not before she caught a glimpse of what looked like a soda bottle resting against her door. As she moved back toward the window, she mentally filled in the blanks as to what had happened.

Someone had cut a hole in her window and tossed in a Molotov cocktail. Would he be waiting on her when she was forced to leave the room?

Smoke thickened, closing her lungs and burning her eyes. Light-headed, she forced back the panic and sent prayers heavenward. She didn't have a choice.

She stood and shoved the window up. Fresh cold air blew in and she sucked in a lungful, but she didn't climb out as she considered her options.

Her hesitation saved her as a gunshot shattered the window just above her head. Heart pounding, she ducked back to the floor and lifted the phone. "Officer in trouble. I need help now!"

"Help is en route, ma'am."

"How far away?"

"Two minutes."

"I don't have that long!" She took a shallow breath of the air near the floor. *Just keep breathing. Don't pass out.*

Nothing to do but get out. And not through her bedroom door. Or the bedroom window. On hands and knees, she spun, her brain whirling. The bathroom. Flames crept toward the door. Once she went in, she wasn't coming out. Katie took a deep breath, coughed until she thought she might lose a lung and darted inside. She slammed the door shut and raced toward the window.

She pushed it up and kicked the screen out of the way.

Smoke filled the bathroom and stars danced before her eyes even as another breath of fresh air wafted over her. With a prayer on her lips, she gripped the window-sill and hauled herself over. As she hit the bushes below, she heard the crack of a gunshot and felt the bite of the bullet.

Six

Jordan heard the gunshot as he stepped out of his car. His heartbeat kicked into overdrive. "Cort!"

Cort was already racing for the back of the house. The next crack came seconds later. Jordan came to the edge of the house, weapon in hand, wrists pressed to his chest, the muzzle of the gun aimed toward the night sky. With one swift move, he swung around. And found the area empty.

But Katie's house on fire.

"Katie!" Jordan flinched at the sight of the flames roaring from her bedroom window. "Oh, no," he whispered. "Katie!"

The moon revealed a dark figure running the length of the back fence, a rifle clutched in his left hand. Cort bolted after him while Jordan raced toward the broken window of Katie's bedroom. Smoke gushed from the opening and he couldn't get close. Terror shot through him. *No, God, no. Don't let it be. Please, Lord.*

He heard the sirens coming. But it was too late. There was no way Katie would survive. He sank to his knees as firefighters rounded the house and turned their hoses on the blaze. He knew more were out front doing the same.

Movement caught his attention. He turned, weapon ready — and nearly dropped it in shock. "Katie!"

She stumbled toward him, face pale, blood soaking her left arm. He raced to her, yelling, "I need a paramedic!"

Then, worried no one would hear him over the roar of the water, he scooped her up and headed for the front of the house. Her head lolled against his shoulder. "I'm okay," she whispered. "I think it looks worse than it is." A deep cough racked her and Jordan held her even tighter. "Hurts to breathe." Her rasp told him she'd inhaled her share of smoke.

He was as worried about that as he was the wound in her left shoulder.

Jordan raced to the nearest ambulance. Two paramedics leaped from the vehicle. "Set her on the gurney." Tall, with wavy blond hair pulled into a functional ponytail, a woman who looked to be in her mid-thirties was the first to speak. Her confident, professional manner gave Jordan a small measure of relief. He laid Katie on the gurney just as Cort rushed up.

"He got away. Had a motorcycle stashed just up the road. She all right?"

Jordan stepped back out of the way as the paramedics took over, however, he didn't take his eyes from her still form. "I'm not sure." Anxiety twisted his insides. "What happened? How'd he get past you?"

Cort swiped a gloved hand over his salt-and-pepper hair. "He knew I was here and set up a distraction. I heard a bunch of pops. Turned out to be a whole string of firecrackers about two doors up." Cort's lips tightened and his jaw flexed. "I went to investigate and I guess he slipped around to the back of the house while my attention was diverted." Cort gave a disgusted sigh and muttered, "Can't believe I fell for that. As soon as I saw those things popping in the street, I knew what he'd done. I raced back and saw you climbing out of the car." He looked at Jordan and frowned. "What are you doing here, anyway? How'd you know there was trouble?"

"I didn't. I was going to come tell you to go home since I couldn't sleep." He stepped back up and grasped Katie's hand. Her eyes flickered and she shoved aside the oxygen mask with her good hand. The fact that she was conscious encouraged him.

He looked at the paramedic. "What's your name?"

"Christine."

"How is she?"

Christine moved the mask back into place. "She needs to be checked out by a doctor and get that wound on her shoulder stitched up. The bullet dug a nice groove, but missed anything major. CSU will probably find the bullet embedded somewhere inside."

Thankfulness washed over him. She wasn't hurt as badly as he'd feared. Jordan squeezed her hand. "I'll follow in my car."

He looked back to see Faith Nelson step out of the CSU van. She spotted him and rushed over. "Is Katie all right?"

He nodded to the ambulance. "She's okay for now. She's headed over to the hospital to get checked out." He shook his head. "He shot at her. There are bullets in there somewhere."

Faith looked at the house and the firefighters who worked hard to put out the blaze. "Might be a while before I can get in there to look."

"Yeah."

"But I'll find the bullets if they're in there."

"I'd be interested to know if they match the ones from the diner."

"She's stable," Christine told him. "We're ready to transport her."

"She needs a bodyguard." He had an idea. He dialed Gregory Lee's number. In short, concise sentences, he filled the man in. "Can you meet us at the hospital? Do you have anyone that can watch out for her?"

"Yeah. We've got buddies who'll take vacation days if they have to to help keep her safe."

Jordan had figured that would be the case. "Thanks. I'm on the way to the hospital with her now. Uniformed officers are on the scene. Some are searching for the shooter, others are going door to door telling the neighbors what happened and to lock up tight until this guy is caught."

"Good." A pause. "Does this have to do with her sister's case?"

"It's looking more and more like it."

"Man." A sigh filtered through the line. "All right. I'll see you at the hospital."

The ambulance doors slammed shut and Jordan ran to his car and climbed in to follow behind.

Katie woke, drew in a deep breath, choked and gave a ragged, hacking cough. When she opened her watery eyes, she saw Erica on one side of her bed and Jordan on the other. "What's going on?" she rasped.

Erica pushed Katie's hair from her eyes. "You don't remember?"

Katie frowned. The fire. So that's why her throat, her chest, her eyes . . . everything hurt. "I remember. My weapon!"

Jordan said, "We found it behind the bush under your bathroom window. I've got it locked in my glove compartment." He didn't even blink at the fact that her weapon was her first thought. Erica looked slightly bemused, but she had been around law enforcement enough to know no cop wanted their weapon in the hands of the wrong person. Katie must have dropped hers when she fell out of the bathroom window and behind the bushes.

She wilted back against the pillow. "My house . . ."

"Your bedroom is destroyed," Jordan said, "but it looks like they were able to save the rest of it — other than the water damage. Gregory said you kept a copy of all your major personal records at the office. He found your home insurance number and they'll be out there first thing Monday morning."

For some silly reason, Katie felt tears fill

her eyes. She blinked them back. "Thanks. And Mariah?"

"I've filled her in," Erica said. "She said she'd be by to see you soon."

"And these are for you." Jordan reached behind him and picked up a large vase that held a gorgeous bouquet of flowers. "Oh, my," she breathed. "Who are those from?"

Jordan shuffled his feet and she thought she saw a red tint creep into his cheeks. "Me. I thought they'd brighten things up around here."

Her heart skittered, skipped a beat then pounded into overdrive. "They're beautiful. Thank you so much."

He shrugged and ducked his head in a gesture of shyness that touched her. And made her appreciate the gesture all the more because she could tell he was uncomfortable.

Erica cleared her throat and held up Katie's purse. "Your partner found this in the den and brought it for you. It was a little waterlogged, but I think it might survive." She placed another bag on the bed beside Katie. "And these are some clothes for when you leave. I don't think you want anything to do with your wardrobe right now."

"Thank you. That's helpful."

Katie moved and winced at the fire racing

through her shoulder. "He shot at me. Feels like he hit me. How bad is it?"

"Not bad at all." The voice from the door dragged her attention from her visitors. A tall woman with dark skin and even darker eyes approached the bed.

She held out a hand and Katie shook it. "I'm Dr. Sterling." She opened the chart. "You've got a nice wound, and it'll take a while to heal. You've also got about sixteen stitches. We've got you on an antibiotic drip and have treated you for smoke inhalation. That handy little device next to you is a morphine pump for the pain, but we'll give you a prescription you can take at home if you need it. You should be good to go first thing in the morning."

Katie blinked. She'd escaped relatively unscathed. *Thank You, Lord.* Exhaustion swamped her. All she wanted to do was sleep. "No more narcotics," she whispered. "What time is it?"

Jordan glanced at his watch. "Eight forty-five."

"Thursday morning?"

"Yes."

She gasped. "My parents. They'll be worried that I haven't shown up or called or —" She struggled to sit up but Jordan placed a hand on her arm with a glance at the doctor.

"Erica called them."

"Oh." She lay back against the pillow as reality sank in. Her parents knew she was hurt and in the hospital, but they weren't here. Hurt seared her. She would have thought her father would come by even if her mother refused. Then again, maybe it was better if he didn't.

Katie swallowed hard and wondered if she'd ever get to the point where she could just accept her mother's rejection and get on with her life. Maybe. Maybe she would just have to let God's love be enough. But she wasn't sure she knew how to do that.

Even though the pain of her parents' absence swirled within, her eyelids drooped. Dr. Sterling smiled. "Get some rest. I'll check back with you in a few hours."

Erica patted her hand as the door closed. "Why don't you listen to your doctor and get some rest? I'm going to sit here for a while."

"And I'm going to be around," Jordan said.

"What are you doing here? How did you know to show up last night?"

"I couldn't sleep."

"So you thought you'd come watch my house?"

"You need a bodyguard."

She forced herself to focus on him. "And you're taking on that job?" she rasped.

His eyes narrowed, then his face softened. "Can't think of any other job I'd rather do right now."

Katie wanted to respond, but let the drugs and fatigue take over. She felt a smile curve her lips before the darkness crept in.

She opened her eyes at the sound of the knock on the door. Erica was nowhere to be seen. Jordan stood from the chair where he'd been dozing. Katie blinked, wondering how long she'd slept, but noticed with relief she didn't feel so drugged now.

When Jordan opened the door and her father stepped into the room, her heart gave a fast beat of joy. He'd come.

"Katie?" Concern knit his brows almost together at the bridge of his nose. "Are you all right?"

Her father's fifty-six-year-old face had aged a bit since she'd seen him last week. How was it possible to think he had a few more lines around his mouth, a bit more gray in his hair? "Hey, Dad. I'm all right."

He walked over to stand next to her. "Erica called us."

"Us?" She couldn't help it. She looked behind him, but knew her mother wouldn't

101

be there. Katie's mother couldn't be bothered with the daughter who'd let her youngest child be taken. It didn't matter that
Katie had been only fourteen years old. It
didn't matter that she'd been asked by an
adult to help carry groceries into the house.
What her mother couldn't get over was the
fact that Katie simply hadn't made Lucy go
with her. That Katie had taken her eyes off
her sister for approximately ten minutes and
the girl had vanished while on Katie's watch.

Her father cleared his throat. "Me. Your
mother wasn't feeling very well and —"

"You don't have to make excuses for her,
Dad. I get it."

He flushed and shoved his hands deeper
into his pockets. "Yeah. I guess you do."

And that was all that would be said about
it. She sighed as fresh pain ripped through
her. Would her mother never forgive her? "I
sent her some chocolates for her birthday.
Did she get them?"

"She did. And ate every one of them." He
smiled and Katie thought it looked a little
forced. "We enjoyed the meal you sent over,
too. Not necessary, but she appreciated it."

"I just wanted to do something for her.
And you." Only she was getting the feeling
no matter what she did, it would never be
enough. She swallowed hard and motioned

to Jordan. "This is Jordan Gray. He's with Finding the Lost. Jordan, this is Bryce Randall, my father."

The two men shook hands.

"Glad to meet you," Jordan said. He looked from her father to her, his curious, watchful gaze making her want to squirm. If it wouldn't hurt her shoulder too much.

"Thanks for coming, Dad. Hopefully, I'll be out of here pretty soon."

"Does this have to do with a case you're working?"

Her gaze met Jordan's. She wasn't ready to tell her father anything yet. "We don't know for sure. We haven't really had time to figure that out."

He looked at Jordan. "Do you mind if I have a moment alone with Katie?"

"Of course." Jordan moved toward the door, and Katie wanted to protest, grab him back and make him stay right beside her. The panicked need for his presence, his protection, stunned her. This was her dad. She could talk to him. And she certainly didn't need Jordan's protection.

Once Jordan let the door close behind him, her father turned to her and swallowed hard. "Are you still looking for Lucy?"

Katie jerked at her sister's name. It had been so long since she'd heard either parent

say it. She gave a short nod. She wasn't going to be the one to bring it up, but she
wouldn't lie about it either. "Of course I
am."

He sighed and rubbed his eyes. "I thought
so."

Katie fidgeted with the blanket. "Is that a
problem?" She couldn't help the challenge
in her tone.

"It could be." He paused and gripped her
hand. "Maybe you should just . . . let her
go."

Her head snapped up. "Like you and
Mom have let her go?"

He flinched and she wished the words
back. And yet she didn't. His jaw firmed
and his eyes narrowed. "Katie, I'm serious.
She's been gone for fourteen years. She's
probably . . . d-d-dead." Tears appeared and
he blinked them back before they could fall.
He took a deep breath. "Just . . . let her go,
get a life. Find a man who loves you and
give your mom and me some grandkids."
He gave her a faint smile. "I think that
would go a long way toward your mother's
healing."

*I don't deserve to get married, have a child.
Be happy.* She bit her lip on the words,
shocked at how loudly they rang in her
mind. She'd tried falling in love once and

104

he'd died. The whole thing with her fiancé had just reinforced the fact that her purpose here on earth was to find Lucy. Then she could be happy. Maybe even be forgiven. "I can't do that, Dad," she whispered.

His hand reached out and grasped her shoulder. "You have to."

She cried out, the harsh tone and his hard grip on her injured shoulder so out of character. She stared at him through the fog of pain and medication. He jerked back at her cry, the stricken look on his face apology enough.

"Dad, please. Stop. You're scaring me." Not really physically, but she didn't recognize this man. He was usually a man who abhorred violence of any kind, but now he curled his fingers into a fist and punched it into his other palm. Sorrow — and fear? — filled his gaze, and he leaned over and kissed the top of her head. Another shock to her system. He hadn't displayed much affection toward her in the last fourteen years. *Maybe because you haven't let him.* She ignored the taunting voice and pulled back to look up at him. "What is it, Dad? What else is going on? You're not telling me something."

His face paled. "Nothing. I just want to see you happy, Katie. Believe it or not, that's all I want. Let Lucy go."

And then he was gone.

SEVEN

Jordan leaned his forehead against the smooth wall and took a deep breath. He needed to go jogging or put in a good workout in the gym. But Katie came first. It was obvious to him that someone didn't want her — or him — nosing around asking about a fourteen-year-old kidnapping.

Why? And who?

The why was easy to figure out. The who was a little more difficult. Was it the kidnapper himself, afraid of what they might find? Or someone who knew who'd taken Lucy and was protecting the kidnapper?

He slowed and considered the two questions. If it was the kidnapper, how did he even know they were investigating again? The answer to that was the person was someone Katie interacted with on a regular basis. Or was it someone he'd interviewed from the neighborhood?

One thing gave him hope — and scared

him to death. If any of the above were true, that meant the kidnapper was still around. Somewhere close. On the one hand, that was good. On the other, it could mean Lucy was dead and the kidnapper was afraid their digging would bring evidence to light as to his identity.

Jordan paced the length of the hallway in front of Katie's room. The door opened and her father stepped into the hall, nodded to Jordan and turned to walk away. He stopped midstride and spun back to meet Jordan's gaze.

Jordan lifted a brow. "Everything all right?"

A sigh filtered between Bryce Randall's lips as he walked toward Jordan. "No. Not really."

"May I help in some way?"

Mr. Randall rubbed his palms against his khaki-clad thighs. "How close are you to Katie? How much influence do you have with her?"

Jordan grunted. "Not much, I'm afraid."

The man's face fell. "Oh."

"Why?"

He blew out a sigh and blinked as though holding back tears. "I want her to stop looking for Lucy."

Not what he'd expected to hear. "Again, why?"

Mr. Randall rubbed a hand over his lips. His nails had been chewed to the quick and a fine tremble ran through his fingers. "Look, it's been fourteen years. If Katie keeps letting this . . . obsession . . . control her life, pretty soon she's not going to have a life. And I really don't want to lose another daughter."

Jordan shoved his hands in his pockets and rocked back on his heels. "I see."

"Do you?"

"Yes. I think I do. I don't want her in danger any more than you do."

Bryce's shrewd eyes narrowed. "You might not have a lot of influence with her, but she means something to you, doesn't she?"

"She's . . . a friend. As well as a partner. Of sorts."

"Uh-huh."

Jordan changed the subject. "Where's Katie's mother? I would think she'd want to be with Katie at this time."

Bryce Randall winced. "Katie's mother isn't well. Hasn't been since Lucy disappeared." He swallowed hard. "In some ways I lost my wife that day, too." He drew in a shuddering breath. "If I lose Katie, I won't live through it and neither will her mother."

A debate raged in Jordan's head. Should he say what he was thinking or keep quiet? His mouth made up his mind. "Katie really needs to hear that from you."

"I told her. Sort of."

"But more importantly, I think she needs to hear it from her mother." Jordan debated whether to say anything more, then went for it. "She's trying to win her mother's love back. She thinks constantly doing for you and her mother is the way to get her to love her again."

Raw pain glittered from the man's eyes. "I know. And that's a topic for another day. For now, please, do your best to convince Katie it's time to let Lucy go. To let her rest in peace."

"Then you think she's dead?"

Bryce's sad eyes met his. "Don't you?"

Katie wanted nothing more than to crawl in bed and shut the world out. Between Gregory and Jordan, they'd made sure she had ample security for her overnight stay at the hospital.

Though she had been sure that Wednesday night would never end, Thursday morning had finally come. And so had the doctor, followed by the nurse bearing her discharge papers. Now she sat in the passenger seat of Jordan's car and pulled the seat belt across her shoulder to click into place. "I could have gotten Erica to come get me."

"I know. She offered, but I told her I wanted to take you home."

Curious, she looked at him. "Why? You have something more about Lucy's case?"

"Maybe, but that's not the only reason."

"What else?" Katie thought she saw a light shade of red bloom on Jordan's cheeks and blinked, sure she must have imagined it. "What else?"

He glanced at her. "Because I wanted to be with you."

Katie swallowed hard. "Oh."

He gave a restrained laugh. One without humor. "Come on, Katie, I know we're working together, but you've got to admit there's a certain . . . something . . . between us." He pulled out of the parking lot, his eyes active, roaming between all the mirrors, and she knew he was worried about being followed.

"A something?" she asked.

"A something."

"Ooookay."

"Now, we can either address it. Or ignore it."

Katie chewed on her lip, flashes of the

confrontation with his father at the morgue running through her mind. "I'm hungry."

Jordan gave a half laugh, half groan. "Okay. We're going to ignore it, then?"

"For now."

"Right. What are you in the mood for?"

"A cheeseburger. A good one, not a frozen one."

"How about Randy's?" Her stomach growled, and he shot her a smile. "I guess that was approval."

"Definitely." His smile sent her heart pounding in a wild dance, her pulse skittering, the butterflies fluttering in the pit of her stomach. Even though she was afraid to acknowledge the attraction to him, she couldn't very well deny it to herself.

But it scared her.

And thrilled her all at the same time.

But she wasn't going to do anything about it yet. She still had to find Lucy and couldn't let her feelings distract her.

Besides, his parents hated her.

He pulled into the parking lot at Randy's and she climbed out of the car, moving slowly in order not to tear her stitches.

"You were very lucky, you know." He stared at her shoulder.

"I'm not sure I attribute it to luck." She touched the bandage. "Right now, I'm giving God the credit."

"Yeah."

They entered the restaurant with Jordan watching her back. Katie kept her eyes open for anything that made her uneasy. The smell of grilling burgers and fried potatoes greeted her, making her stomach growl once more. She licked her lips, ready to eat. She didn't mind hospital food, but there was no way she was going to turn down Randy's burgers.

Once settled, she set the menu aside, already knowing her order. "What are you getting?"

"I'll get what I always get. Breakfast. Eggs, bacon, grits and sometimes a steak. But the grits are my favorite. I don't know what Randy does to those grits, but I've yet to find anyone to match him for the flavor."

"You come here a lot?"

"Weekly. Sometimes daily. And I always get the grits."

She laughed as the waitress approached with their water. She gave a flirtatious wink at Jordan. "It's been a while since you've been in, Jordan. Good to see you haven't forgotten us." She turned to Katie and gave her a sweet smile. "What can I get you?"

Once they'd given their order, Katie leaned back with a grimace.

"Sore?" Jordan asked.

"In spades."

His lips tightened. "I should have taken you home."

"And miss Randy's? Not a chance." She sipped her water. "I'm on medical leave for the next week," she said softly.

"Why do I get the feeling you have something other than resting and healing on your agenda?"

She lifted a brow. "Nothing gets past you, does it?"

He smiled at her. Within a few minutes, their food was in front of them. Jordan paused like he might be waiting on her to say a blessing. Even as disappointed with God as she was, she found she couldn't ignore Him. He still gave her hope and she found strength in leaning on His promises.

So she still prayed, and she still wanted to say grace over her food. Katie bowed her head and Jordan followed her cue. His low voice reached her ears. "Lord, we thank You for this food and for Katie's safety. Please guide us as we continue to search for Lucy. Let us bring her kidnapper to justice and give her family closure. Amen."

"Amen," she whispered. "Thanks."

Katie dug into her burger. The first bite sent her taste buds dancing. They ate in silence until Jordan's phone rang. He glanced at the number and set his fork down. "Hello?" He listened, the furrow between his brows easing as he nodded. "Great. Great. Thanks so much." He hung up.

"What was that all about?" Katie asked.

"That was one of your former neighbors I'd managed to track down. She no longer lives in the neighborhood, but she's still friends with Elaine Johnson. I'd left a message for her to call me if she knew anything about Mrs. Johnson. Apparently, Mrs. Johnson is now a resident of White Oak Manor's assisted-living program."

"Oh, what a shame. I guess that means her health is failing."

"Look like that's the case."

"But at least we know where she is now."

"Exactly. I suggest we get over to White Oak as soon as possible and see if she can tell you anything more."

Katie nodded but frowned. "I really don't think there's going to be anything for her to tell me, but I'm ready to give it another go."

"I'm assuming you haven't heard anything back from your sketch artist?"

She blinked and grabbed her phone. "In all the craziness, I forgot to call her back. I saw her number on my phone this morning."

Her phone buzzed, and she snagged it. "Hello, Gregory."

"Hey, just thought I'd let you know that we've got the guy who killed Wesley Wray."

"Who is it?"

"An inmate by the name of Charlie West."

"Did he say why he killed Wesley?"

"Just that Wray was on his last nerve so he decided to get rid of him. Charlie's in for the rest of his life. He had nothing to lose killing Wray."

"Someone paid him to do it. Will you check his family members' bank accounts and see if we can find a money trail to follow?"

"Already thought of that. West is married with kids. His wife just had five grand deposited into her account this morning."

"So that's what a person's life is worth these days," Katie muttered.

Gregory said, "I'll keep you updated as I get information. I'm working on tracking the money."

"Okay, thanks."

She hung up and brought Jordan up to date. He thought about it. "I guess we need to question Mr. West."

"I guess so."

"Then let's —"

His sharply indrawn breath snagged her attention from the phone. "What is it?"

He shot her a look full of apology. "My parents. Heading this way."

Katie's stomach dipped to her toes. The last time she'd seen Paul and Lisa Gray, they'd been staring down at the body of their dead son and blaming her for his death. She swallowed hard, suddenly having to fight to keep the hamburger down.

Jordan fought the knot of dread from in his gut. He shouldn't have brought Katie here. Not when his parents ate here almost as often as he did. What had he been thinking?

His father's eyes lit up when he saw him and he and his mother made their way toward him. And Katie.

His mother's eyes landed on the back of Katie's head and a smile lifted the corners of her lips because she didn't know who Jordan was eating with. Yet. Jordan bit back a groan. He stood, desperate to cut them off.

He stepped forward and held out his hand. His dad shook it while his mother tried to get a glimpse of the woman sharing her son's table.

His father asked, "You're still planning on coming to dinner Sunday, right?"

Jordan nodded. "Yes, I'll be there."

"And who is this lovely —" Lisa's shocked gasp could be heard around the restaurant. Jordan closed his eyes and said a quick prayer. His father frowned and stepped around his wife to see what had her pale and trembling.

"You!"

Katie stood and wiped her mouth with her napkin. She shot Jordan a look full of apology. "Hello." The word trembled on her lips, and he wanted to hug her for the effort.

A strangled sound came from Paul's throat and his wild, stunned gaze landed back on Jordan. "Her? What are you doing here with her? You would sit at the same table with her?"

Jordan saw they had the attention of the restaurant and he rested a hand on his mother's elbow. "Why don't you get a seat? Katie and I were getting ready to leave. I'll come by later and explain everything."

"Explain? What's there to explain? I can see exactly what's going on." With a scathing glance at Katie, Paul took Lisa's elbow. "I won't breathe the same air as her. We'll find somewhere else to eat." He escorted his wife from the restaurant.

Katie sat with a thump, her face pale and

pinched.

Jordan sat across from her and reached for her hand. He squeezed it and she pulled away from him. Still looking at the door where his parents had made their sudden departure, she asked, "Will you please just take me home now? I'm not feeling well."

"Katie, I'm sorry."

"No." She finally looked at him and the anguish there tore at his heart. "It's not your fault."

"It's not anyone's fault but Neil's and the killer who attacked him."

She sighed and pushed her plate aside with a trembling hand. "Just take me home." She blinked. "Then again, I guess home is out of the question. Will you take me to a hotel?"

"I thought Erica said you could stay with her."

"She did, but I refuse to put her and Molly in danger. A hotel will be fine."

Jordan didn't like it, but he nodded and she rose, dug into her purse and dropped a ten-dollar bill on the table. He grabbed it and pushed it back into her hand. "I got this one."

It said a lot about her fragile state of mind when she just took the money and walked to the door without another word.

Jordan almost asked her to stay inside and wait for him before walking to the car, but he didn't have to. She stood by the door, ignoring a few of the still-staring patrons. As the cashier handed him his change, he stole another glance in her direction. She'd squared her shoulders and planted her hands on her hips as she stood to the side of the door and examined the parking lot.

Jordan pocketed the money and walked over to her. "See anything?"

"No. I don't see him, but he's watching."

"All right then, let's go find him."

EIGHT

Katie set her small bag of borrowed clothes on the sofa. She looked around. "It's a nice room."

A small suite, it had a mini kitchen that opened into a sitting area complete with a full-size couch and a flat-screen television. The work area was next to the sliding glass doors that led to a small balcony. A king-size bed and bathroom in a separate room rounded out the suite.

Jordan went through it as though he thought her attacker would be waiting. He'd retrieved her weapon and the comforting weight of it at the small of her back allowed her to breathe a little easier. Using the shoulder holster was out of the question with her injury.

She glanced at the clock on the micro-wave. Twelve forty-five. It felt like it should be a.m., not p.m.

"Cort will be watching your room tonight," Jordan said as he walked back into the main living area. "He feels guilty for letting that guy get so close to you."

"It wasn't his fault."

"He doesn't feel that way."

"I really don't think there was anything he could have done differently."

"That's what I keep telling him." His phone rang. "Hello?"

Katie placed the rescued file on the desk and started pulling the papers out one at a time as she listened to his side of the conversation.

"Thanks, Max." Jordan hung up. "Max said he parked your car four doors down from your room."

"Good."

"He also said he doesn't think he was followed, but can't vouch for that a hundred percent."

"I trust him."

"But you'll still give the car the once-over before you get in it, right?"

She lifted a brow. "Of course." Katie turned her attention back to the papers. "They're dry now. Might be a little hard to read, but . . ."

"You really don't need the file at this point, do you?"

He took a seat at the table.

She shrugged. "No. The only thing I didn't have memorized was your notes, but I read them."

"I've got copies." He paused. "I'm sorry about my parents."

Pain darted through her. She met his gaze for a brief moment, then dropped her eyes to the file. "You don't have to apologize for them. They're entitled to their pain."

"But they're not entitled to lash out at you."

"They have to have someone to blame. I suppose I'm the best choice for that. I arrested their son and he died." She paused then asked, "Do they even acknowledge the fact that he was drinking and driving?"

"No. They're convinced it was all just a mistake, a misunderstanding." She stared at him and he shrugged with a sad frown. "They're not in touch with reality when it comes to Neil's death."

"Have you tried to tell them?"

He gave her a shuttered look. "I've tried. A little."

She gave a trembling sigh. "Why don't you feel the same as your parents?"

He flushed and shook his head. "I did for a while. But working with you, even in a limited capacity, on Molly James's kidnapping transformed my opinion of you. I re-

123

alized for the first time that you weren't some egotistical cop who had something to prove by teaching a drunk kid a lesson. You can't predict the future. You put a drunk man in a cell with other drunks. It happens every day. It's what cops do."

"I know, I just wish . . ." she rasped. Emotion choked her almost as much as the smoke she'd inhaled. She cleared her throat and stood, walked to the window and placed herself to the side so she could see out, but anyone watching wouldn't be able to see her. The parking lot was half full. No one loitering in the shadows that she could tell.

"And —"

When he broke off, she looked at him. "And?"

"And there's stuff about Neil they don't know." He glanced away, then back. "Stuff I haven't told them."

She lifted a brow. "Like what?"

"It doesn't matter at this point. Suffice it to say I'm not sure I'm doing them a favor and am praying about it."

Completely baffled, she stared at him. He shook his head. "Never mind."

Okay, then. When — if — he decided to share with her whatever he was talking about, she'd listen. Until then . . . Katie asked, "What about this neighbor, Mrs.

McKinney? I talked to her twice but didn't get much."

At first he didn't answer and she wondered if he was ready to change the subject. She let out a small breath of relief when he did. Talking about Neil and his parents caused a hard knot to form in her stomach. She needed to talk about something different. He finally said, "She'd brought her husband home from the doctor about three hours after Lucy disappeared. When they got home, they saw all the commotion, but no one really talked to them because they weren't there when it happened. I thought about going to see her." He shrugged. "And while I doubt she can tell us anything, I don't want to leave any stone unturned."

She nodded. "First I have a stop to make."

"Where to?"

"I want to go see Frank and ask him a couple of questions. He told me to come see him at four, but I'm going to see if he'll be willing to just talk to me if I walk in. If he's there."

"Ah." He pursed his lips and looked like he might argue the wisdom of that. Instead, he stood and she followed him down the steps to his car. "I'm going to hunt down Tracy, too, and see if she's got a composite of our shooter."

As she slid into the passenger seat, she supposed she ought to get her own vehicle. In fact she was quite surprised at her rather passive agreement in letting him be her chauffeur. The truth was, she liked the man. Liked being with him, liked his sense of humor, liked bouncing the case off of him and getting his feedback.

And that worried her. Jordan was very easy to be around, but somewhere in his eyes, there was a pain that never really went away. She wondered about it. Wondered if he'd ever share it with her.

Then wondered why she wanted him to. They had no future together. His parents had already lost one son because of her. There was no way she'd cause them any more pain by falling in love with the other.

"You okay?"

He pulled her out of her disturbing thoughts and she nodded, turning to stare out the window. "Just thinking."

"Yeah. I know what you mean."

Her phone rang. Gregory. "Hey."

"Hey. I tracked the money that landed in West's account."

"Great. Where'd it come from?"

"It was a cash deposit, so I don't have a name, just a video snapshot of the guy who made the deposit. Trying to get a name to match the face."

"Send the face to Jordan's phone. He can use his resources with the FBI and put their facial recognition software to good use."

Jordan nodded. Within seconds, his phone dinged and he pulled over to shoot the email to his buddy at the FBI. Katie hung up with Gregory feeling like they were making baby steps, but at least they weren't going backward.

The rest of the drive to the station didn't take long. Jordan drove with practiced ease while Katie kept her gaze glued to the mirrors.

"You see anyone that makes you twitchy?"

"No. Not yet."

"Me, either."

"Doesn't mean he's not there," she muttered.

"Yeah."

He pulled into the parking lot, and Katie stared at the building that had become her second home. "Should have just brought a sleeping bag and slept in my office."

He laughed. "Might be the safest place in the city for you."

She shook her head and climbed out of the vehicle. Katie led the way into the station, eyes scanning the familiar area. Fellow officers called out well wishes and a few even offered hugs. Jordan tapped her arm. "I'm going to be in the evidence room. I want to take a look at the original file on Lucy again."

"There's nothing in it that you haven't seen. I copied everything."

He shrugged. "You're probably right, but I just want to take a look."

"Sure." Katie passed her desk and went straight to Frank's.

He looked up and jerked in surprise. "Hey, I didn't expect to see you."

"We had a four o'clock appointment, remember?"

"Yes, of course. I just figured after last night . . ." He shrugged. "Glad you're okay." He glanced at his watch. "It's not four."

"I know." She smiled. "Do you have few minutes? I've got some other things I need to do. I'm not planning on coming back here after I leave, so I would appreciate it if you'd just talk to me now."

"You still want to go over your sister's case?"

"If you don't mind. I have a question or two I still need answered."

He sighed. "Have a seat."

Katie sat and reached in her bag to pull out Lucy's file. She opened it on the desk in front of her and turned it so it was right side up for Frank. She pointed to the small slip of paper with the diner's address. "Jordan and I went here yesterday and talked to the owner. It's also where we were shot at."

Frank frowned at her. "You've had a rough couple of days."

"I have, but that's not important right now. I talked to Betty June Clark, and she said she remembers the case. And the two detectives who worked it."

"Really?" He leaned back and crossed his arms. Then sat forward. "Wait a minute, I remember her. Pretty blonde?"

"Yes."

He nodded. "She thought the kidnapper had come in with Lucy and eaten there. Called us to check it out."

"Right."

"At the time, there were no surveillance cameras working. The place was pretty rundown. We talked to her and the other workers, but came up with pretty much nothing."

"What about the hair in the bathroom?"

"What hair?"

Impatience licked at her. "Betty said the girl had chopped hair and she found hair around the toilet in the men's bathroom. Said she told you and Danny Jackson about it."

"Yes, I remember something about that, but if I remember correctly, it had already been cleaned up by the time we got in there." He rubbed his eyes. "Come on, Katie, it's been fourteen years. I haven't looked at that case since we filed it with cold cases." He spread his hands, palms up, in a helpless gesture. "I can't remember everything."

She held her temper in check. He was right. It had been a long time. "Then maybe you remember this. Why wasn't your visit there documented in the folder?"

He frowned. "It was. Both Danny and I filled out reports."

She tapped the file. "Nothing but that little scrap of paper with the address."

He sighed and rubbed his eyes. "I don't know, Katie, you know how it is. You have ten cases going at the same time and sometimes things might . . ." He trailed off.

"Slip through the cracks?" she asked softly, her tone deadly.

"No, no, not that, just — you're talking fourteen years ago."

She got up before she said something she shouldn't.

"Katie, stop. Come on. I didn't mean we didn't do our jobs. We did. We wrote the reports. I don't know why they're not in the file."

She kept her back to him and took a deep breath. "If you remember, give me a call, will you?"

"Of course."

"Thanks." She started to leave then turned back. "Have you seen Tracy?"

"Uh . . . yeah. She was near the break room right before you came over."

She left, the file clutched tight, thankful it hadn't been destroyed in the fire.

Katie had another idea. She found Jordan in the break room studying the file. "Find anything?"

"Nothing really. You?"

She shook her head and took a deep breath. "I've had this feeling before, but today sealed it."

"What feeling?"

"That the investigation was botched. Whatever word you want to use, Frank Miller and Danny Jackson did my sister and my family an injustice."

He frowned. "What did he say about the diner?"

She told him. "I want to go talk to his former partner, Danny Jackson."

"He's on my list, but I haven't talked to him yet."

"I talked to him briefly about a year ago, but he was more interested in his golfing handicap than he was in rehashing a cold case."

"That's unusual. Most retired guys relish talking about their cases."

"Yeah, the cases they've solved. Not the ones that got away."

"True." He closed the file. "You were right. You copied every last teeny, tiny piece of information in this file, didn't you?"

"I did."

He stood. "Let me put this back and we can go."

"I'm going to see if I can find Tracy." She told him where the woman's office was.

He said, "I'll meet you there."

Katie left him to return the file and headed down a long hallway and to the second floor. She leaned against the wall to catch her breath and realized her lungs still hadn't fully recovered from her bout with the fire. The burning in her shoulder was aggravating, but nothing she couldn't ignore. Once she got her breath, she knocked on the door.

"Come in."

Katie stepped inside to see Tracy at her desk, phone pressed to her ear. When she saw Katie, she hung up. "I was just dialing your number." She frowned with concern. "How are you feeling?"

"Like I need an oxygen tank strapped to my back, but other than that, I'm all right."

"Have you heard anything back about the fire? How it started?"

"A Molotov cocktail through my bedroom window."

"Ouch." Her friend winced. "You've made someone a little angry?"

"Yeah, a little."

"Who?"

"I've no idea." She didn't want to discuss the fire or the fact that someone wanted her dead. "Hey, do you have the composite for the shooter at the diner? Bobby Young is our witness."

Tracy blinked at her. "No, I don't have it. He never came in, and he hasn't answered my calls."

Unease crawled up Katie's spine. "What do you mean he never came? He was coming as soon as he could after he got his car towed, got checked out at the hospital and changed his clothes. I think he had some blood on them and wanted to change. You're saying he didn't come over?"

"Right. I left a message on your voice mail at home yesterday morning." She grimaced. "Which means you probably didn't get it."

"No. It's been so crazy, I haven't even called to check my messages. Why didn't you leave one on my cell?"

"I started to, but the captain walked in just as I went to voice mail, so I just hung up. I figured you'd get the message at home anyway. Or see my number and call me. Which you did."

Katie nodded. "Thanks. I'm going to find Jordan and we'll see if we can track down Mr. Young." As she talked, she backed toward the door. And came up against what felt like a brick wall. She spun to find herself nose to chin with Jordan. His hands came up to cup her elbows. She jerked back and he gave her a crooked smile. But the glint in his narrowed eyes said he'd enjoyed the brief proximity.

Her pounding heart said she had, too.

Not going to happen, Katie, remember? His parents hate you.

She took a deep breath and filled Jordan in on the latest. His half smile dipped into full frown. "You have his address?"

She turned and looked at Tracy. "You have it?"

Tracy turned back to her computer and with a few clicks of her keyboard, she had Bobby Young's driver's license on the screen. Another click sent her printer humming. She handed the paper to Katie.

"Thanks."

"When you find him," Tracy said, "let me know."

"Count on it."

Katie walked beside Jordan as they headed down the steps and toward the exit. "Will you take me to pick up my car?"

"Now?"

"Yes. I prefer to have it."

"You sure you're feeling all right? You just got out of the hospital. You were shot, remember?"

She shot him a sardonic look. "Really? And besides, it was just a graze."

He gave a short laugh and said, "Sure."

In Jordan's car, as they headed back to the hotel, Katie's phone buzzed. "Hi, Erica."

"Hey, how are you feeling?"

"I've felt better, but I'm doing all right."

"Max and I want you and Jordan to come to dinner tonight. Do you think you can make it?"

"I don't know. I don't think that's very safe for you."

"It will be if you just make sure you're not followed."

Katie sighed. "You know I can't guarantee that."

"You don't want to stay here — I get that.

But I think coming to eat will be fine."

Uneasiness twisted Katie's stomach into a knot. She probably should say no, but she hadn't seen Erica in a while and would love to spend time with her and Molly. But Erica wasn't finished. "I want to discuss your case, anyway. Might as well do it here as at the office."

"We're on our way to talk to a witness from the wreck."

"Then come after. It's all right if it's late. I'll get Molly settled with her favorite movie so we can talk uninterrupted."

Katie caved. "All right, then, let me ask Jordan." He glanced at her and she relayed the invitation. He nodded. "We'll be there," Katie said. "I'll call you when I'm on the way."

"Great. See you when you get here."

Katie gnawed on her lower lip. When a warm finger reached over to pull it from the clench of her upper front teeth, shivers ran through her. Jordan glanced at the traffic light then back to her. "You're going to chew right through it if you're not careful."

She swallowed hard and then gathered her wits as he pulled into the hotel parking lot. She grabbed her keys and said, "I'll meet you there."

"Watch your back."

"I always do."

Ten minutes later, she pulled behind Jordan to the curb of Bobby Young's house. As far as she could tell, no one had followed.

The clock pushed toward two o'clock. She climbed from the car and looked around. Jordan approached and she asked, "I didn't see anyone following, did you?"

"Not a soul."

"That almost makes me nervous."

"I understand that completely."

Mr. Young's neighborhood was on a cul-de-sac with five other houses. Large lots and a lot of trees gave it a feeling of privacy and community at the same time. Katie nodded. "Nice place."

"Very."

Jordan walked up the steps to the porch of the traditional ranch and rang the bell. Katie kept an eye on the area around them. Right now, she didn't like being too exposed. The middle of her back between her shoulders itched.

No one answered the door.

"Not answering his phone, not answering the door. How old is he?" Katie asked.

"Sixty-four."

"He could be working or retired. Do we know?"

"I have his statement on my phone. Let

me see if that information came up. Hold on a second." He pressed a few buttons. "Retired."

"Retired usually means not at work, but never at home if the retiree is in good health and active." She pointed to the flag hanging from the porch. "A golfer's flag. Might be on the course. We have another number for him?"

"Nope. That's his cell phone. He doesn't have a landline."

Katie pursed her lips and walked to the garage. The double door was closed, but had four windows at the top. "I'm too short to see in. Wanna take a look?"

Jordan obliged. "A single car parked on the right side closest to the entry to the house. It's not the car from the wreck. Can't see the tags, but I'm willing to bet it's a rental."

"Then if his car is in the garage, why isn't he answering the door or his phone?"

Before Jordan could answer, his phone rang. He listened for a few minutes then hung up. Katie lifted a brow in silent question. Jordan said, "We got a hit on the guy at the bank who made the deposit into West's wife's account."

"Who is it?"

"A guy by the name of Norman Rhames."

"Never heard of him."

"Apparently he's got some ties to a terrorist group, but basically keeps his nose clean except for crimes that don't keep him behind bars for very long."

"We need to track down this Mr. Rhames and find out who had him deposit that money."

"Help you folks?"

Jordan turned to see a well-groomed lady in her mid-seventies standing in the drive next to Mr. Young's. She shut her mailbox and headed their way.

Jordan said, "We're looking for Mr. Young."

"He should be there. Although I didn't see him take his usual morning walk."

"He walks every day at the same time?" Katie asked.

"Pretty near every day. He's got a touch of arthritis but even when it's acting up, he doesn't let it keep him down for long." She pushed her glasses a little farther up on her nose. "You're not his daughter, are you?"

Katie said, "No, ma'am. I'm Detective Katie Randall with the police department. Mr. Young was involved in a wreck a couple of days ago. We just needed to ask him a few more questions." She flashed her badge and the woman placed a hand over her heart.

"He told me about that when he got home. He looked awful. I'd come outside for a short walk, and he pulled into the drive. His son Hunter picked him up from the hospital. Bobby had blood all over his clothes and everything. I asked if he needed anything and he said no, he just wanted to change and get to the police station. He'd seen the carjacker and needed to meet with the sketch artist. Sounded like something right off the television."

So he'd arrived home from the hospital and had planned to meet with Tracy.

"You're pretty good friends then?"

The woman smiled, her white teeth straight and even. "I'm Janice McDowell. And yes, Bobby and I are friends as well as neighbors. We try to look out for each other since we both live alone."

"How did Mr. Young plan to get to the police station?" Katie asked.

"He has another car. It was his wife's. He's never been able to sell it. Thankfully he wasn't hurt more than a scratch and a couple of bruises. And that carjacking! Why, what this world is coming to —" She shook her head.

"Do you have Hunter's number?" Katie asked.

"I might have it somewhere. Would take me a while to find it, probably." She looked at the phone in Jordan's left hand. "Or you could look it up on that fancy toy of yours. I even know the name of his street because it's my daughter's name. Laurel Street."

"Hunter Young. Laurel Street. Got it." Jordan hit dial. "Nate, hey, I need some information." Jordan had bypassed the white pages and gone straight to his information specialist at Quantico. Nate gave him what he needed within seconds. Jordan dialed the number that flashed up in his text message box.

"Hunter Young."

"Hi, Mr. Young, this is Special Agent Jordan Gray with the FBI. I met your father when he was involved with the wreck a couple of days ago." Had it only been two days? "He was supposed to come down to the police station to meet with a sketch artist, but he never showed up and we're having trouble getting in touch with him."

Silence greeted him.

"Mr. Young?"

"I'm just thinking. I'm working at home today. I can run over and check on him and let you know."

"We're actually at his house."

"Oh. Stay there, I'm on the way."

Jordan hung up and passed on the information.

"Oh, dear. I do hope everything is all right."

Katie gave the woman a reassuring smile. "We can let you know if you'd like to wait in the comfort of your home."

"That's a very nice way of saying I need to stay out of the way, hmm?"

Katie gave a low chuckle. "Yes, ma'am."

Mrs. McDowell nodded and gave a light laugh, but it didn't cover her worried glance at Bobby Young's house.

"Does he have any animals?" Katie asked.

She shook her head. "No. He likes to travel too much. Said an animal would tie him down."

"Thank you, Mrs. McDowell, you've been very helpful."

"Please let me know when you talk to him?"

"Of course. We'll have him call you."

She nodded and walked slowly back up her driveway.

Jordan looked at Katie. "I'm going to walk around to the back and see if I see anything."

Katie nodded. Jordan headed around the

side of the house but turned back at the sound of a vehicle approaching. A classy white convertible Mercedes with a black top. Hunter Young must do well for himself. The Mercedes pulled to the curb and a tall man in his early forties climbed from the car. A worried frown creased his forehead. "I'm Hunter Young."

Jordan shook the man's outstretched hand. "FBI Special Agent Jordan Gray. This is Detective Katie Jacobs."

He blanched. "Since when does the FBI investigate a car wreck?"

Katie flashed her badge and said, "He was with me working another case when it happened. He's not officially investigating, but we were both concerned when your father didn't show up like he promised, so thought we'd check on him."

Hunter nodded. "You've every reason to be concerned. If Dad said he'd be there, he would have been. I brought him home from the hospital, and that's all he talked about. Once all the excitement was over and everyone was okay, he thought it all a great adventure. He was excited about working with the sketch artist to find the guy responsible." Hunter walked toward the house, pulling a set of keys from his pocket. "I tried calling his cell all the way over here. He rarely doesn't answer. And usually calls me right back if I do get his voice mail." He opened the front door. Cold air rushed out at them. "Dad?"

Jordan had a bad feeling growing in his gut. Why was the house so cold? It was the middle of December. Everyone had the heat on. Especially with the temps dropping into the low teens at night. He placed a hand on the man's arm. "Do you mind waiting here and letting us check it out?"

"Yes, I mind." He stepped inside. "Dad?" He looked at them. "Why is it so cold in here?" He gave a shudder. "He didn't say anything about the heat pump giving him trouble. Dad?"

"Sir," Katie said. "If we find something, this could be a crime scene. We need to keep it as undisturbed as possible. Wait here."

Her words were an order. Hunter flinched, but stopped in his tracks. "Crime scene? You think —"

"I don't think anything," Katie said with a more gentle tone. "I just want to cover all my bases. For your father's sake."

Hunter swallowed hard and Jordan could tell the man wanted to go tearing through the house. He didn't blame him. If it were his father, he'd feel the same way. But Hunter stood still and clenched a fist. "He could be lying hurt or sick. Hurry. Please."

Katie stepped lightly, wishing for crime scene booties. Bobby Young might not even be here, but her gut cried out that he was and it wasn't going to be good. She stepped into the den and noticed the wide-open French doors that led to the back deck. Cold air blew in.

"Jordan."

"Kitchen's clear." He came up beside her. Spotted the doors. "Uh-oh."

"Mr. Young?" Katie called. They cleared the first floor, then headed for the second. "Bedroom one, clear," she called.

"Bedroom two, clear," Jordan echoed.

Katie stepped into the next room and came to a halt. Even through her heavy down coat, she felt the cold in the house to her bones.

This was his office. The desk faced the window, looking out to the wooded area behind the house. Katie stepped closer and walked around for a view of the chair.

Katie sucked in a deep breath and dropped her chin to her chest in despair. "Jordan!"

She heard his footsteps on the hardwood. "What is it?"

"I found Mr. Young."

NINE

Jordan hated this part of the job. And this wasn't even officially his job. But Katie had asked him to do it while she secured the scene. She already had a crime scene unit and the medical examiner on the way as well as uniformed officers who would canvass the neighborhood, questioning everyone they could find.

When Jordan escorted Hunter from the house and told him the news, the man broke down, his sobs heart wrenching. Jordan didn't blame him. He simply stood there, hand on Hunter's shoulder, until the man could gain some control.

It didn't take him long. Jordan had a feeling Hunter's personality wouldn't let him be emotional for any extended period of time. Within minutes Hunter had wiped his face with his expensive silk tie and hardened his features. Pure fury now blazed from his green eyes. "Who did this?"

Jordan had his suspicions. Unfortunately, he didn't have a name to go with those suspicions. "I don't know, sir, but I promise we'll find out." He paused. "Did your father have any enemies that you know of?"

Appalled, Hunter looked at him. "No. None."

"Did you notice anyone following you home from the hospital?"

Hunter blinked. "No."

And why would he? He had no reason to even think about being followed.

Jordan nodded and as law enforcement arrived. He asked Hunter a few more questions, then did his best to fade into the background. After all, this wasn't his case.

He had to keep reminding himself of that. His case was Katie's case. And while he had a feeling Mr. Young's murder had everything to do with the fact that he'd seen the shooter from the diner, Jordan wasn't going to put his nose any further into the investigation unless he was invited.

He sent a text message to Erica to let her know what was going on. She shot one back.

Come when you can.

An hour later, Katie emerged from the house and veered toward the Mercedes, where Hunter was sitting. He got out of the vehicle, shoulders stooped and looking shell-shocked, his initial fury overshadowed by his crushing grief. For the time being. The anger would return. Jordan knew this from experience.

His phone rang and he recognized the number as the McKinneys'. "Special Agent Gray."

"Hello, Mr. Gray, this is Eileen McKinney. You left a message for me to call you."

"Yes, ma'am. Thanks for calling me back."

Jordan explained what he wanted and Mrs. McKinney clucked. "I don't know what more I can tell. I told that detective the day of the kidnapping everything I could think of — and trust me, that wasn't much."

"I understand, but sometimes talking to a different person can spark something."

"Well, if you want to come on out, I'll be here for the next forty-five minutes or so."

Jordan hesitated, then said, "I'll be there in about fifteen minutes."

"I'll be looking for you."

Jordan hung up. Katie still talked to Hunter, who leaned his head back against the headrest and scrubbed his eyes. He saw Hunter nod, and Katie gave his shoulder a squeeze.

She walked toward him. He said, "You

148

look like you've been hit by a truck. You're not doing yourself any favors by pushing yourself like this. You're supposed to be on leave."

She grimaced. "Tell me what you really think."

"Sorry. I'm concerned." Her gaze warmed for a minute and she looked like she might like to fall into his arms and let him shelter her from the world. He almost held them out to her so she could do it. She blinked and the moment was gone. "You think he was killed by the shooter?"

"I do."

"Because he saw him at the wreck. He was the only one who got a really good look at him, but I'm worried about the others."

"I've contacted my lieutenant, and he's putting extra patrols on the others involved in the wreck. The young mother and the girl, Miranda." She glanced around. "I'm going to be here a little longer. I've got a few more things to take care of. Why don't you head on over to Erica's?"

"I just got a call from Mrs. McKinney. She wants me to come talk to her now."

Hope dusted her expression. "Good. I'll meet you at Erica's as soon as I'm finished here."

"Leave you to come alone? I don't think so."

She rubbed a hand down her face. "Seriously, I'll be fine. I'll get in my car and head over there as soon as we're done. I'm surrounded by cops. The killer is long gone."

Jordan looked around. Strange faces lined the sidewalks, neighbors vying for a glimpse of the action. "You hope."

"I've got the photographer discreetly taking pictures of the crowd. We'll take a look at the pictures and see if anyone jumps out at us. Now go on. I'll be fine."

"I can ask her if tomorrow would be better."

Katie sighed. "Jordan, I've got a job to do. You can't be with me twenty four–seven. Your job is to find out about Lucy. It's what I've hired you to do, not babysit me. I'm a police officer. I'm trained to take care of myself."

Frustration filled him. She was right, but he didn't have to like it.

Gregory stepped from the house. "Katie, can I see you for a minute?"

"Sure." She looked back at Jordan. "Go. I need to know if she has anything to add to Lucy's kidnapping."

Against his better judgment, he nodded. "All right, text me when you're leaving, what route you're taking and anything else I should know."

Katie nodded. "All right. If it will make you feel better."

"It would."

Jordan headed for his car. Reluctantly. But she was right. She was a cop. She was surrounded by cops. He sent up prayer for her safety and pulled away from the scene.

Katie watched Jordan go and prayed he'd come back with some answers. Something. Anything that they could grasp and run with to find Lucy. For the next hour, Katie finished working the crime scene and kept an eye on her back.

By the time she texted Jordan, she was exhausted. All she wanted to do was go to the hotel room and collapse in a heap. In fact, she seriously considered just staying where she was and sleeping in her car.

A tap on her window made her jump. When she saw Gregory's concerned face staring at her, she ordered her pulse to slow down. She lowered the window. "Hey."

"You all right?"

"Hanging in there."

He nodded, his brow still creased. "You heading over to Erica's?"

"I'm thinking about canceling and going

to crawl into bed."

"You need an escort?"

Katie tried to discern if there was any sarcasm in his tone, but didn't detect any. He was concerned. And she was too touchy.

"No. I'll be extra careful."

He pursed his lips. "I like working with you, Katie. See that you stay in one piece, will you?"

She shivered as a gust of cold wind blew across her face. "I'll do my best."

Gregory nodded. "Text me when you're locked in your hotel room, okay?"

Katie smiled. She was glad to know she had people who cared whether she was safe or not. Too bad her parents weren't nearly as concerned. She frowned and ordered herself not to go there. She was tired and didn't need to get maudlin. "Sure."

Gregory walked toward his vehicle and she wondered why the tall, handsome detective didn't spark any romantic interest in her. Immediately Jordan's face came to mind and she knew why she wasn't attracted to Gregory. Jordan was the one who set the butterflies loose in her stomach. He was the one who made her palms sweat and her heart race.

Gregory was a great guy, but he wasn't Jordan.

She sighed and sent a text to Jordan.

I'm going back to the hotel. I'm going to call Erica and tell her I'm not coming.

He replied in a moment.

All right. I'm almost done here. Let me come back and take you back to the hotel.

She ditched the texting and dialed his number. "Hey. You're all the way across town. I'll be at the hotel and locked in my room before you get back here."

"Katie —"

The exasperation in his voice made her smile. She was glad he was concerned. "I'll be fine. I'll text as soon as I get there. I do have a gun, remember? And I'm trained in self-defense. And I'm alert and know some-one's after me. Should be enough, right?"

"Wasn't enough when someone tried to burn your house down, was it?"

Ouch. "Hmm. Okay, I'll give you that point," she muttered. "However, I'm leav-ing now." She pulled away from the curb and waved to Faith as the woman packed her van. The M.E. was still with Bobby Young. Hunter Young had left the scene, claiming he had to go break the news to his family. She didn't envy him that job.

He sighed. "Then stay on the phone with me."

She paused. "All right."

"I'm still going to Erica's. She really wants to talk about this case."

"Fill me in tomorrow?"

"Bright and early. Cort's going to be outside your hotel room all night."

"Poor guy."

"He never sleeps. If he gets four hours a night, he's as fresh as though he's had eight."

"Not fair."

"Tell me about it."

She paused. "Hey, Jordan?"

"Yes."

"Thanks for caring."

"You're welcome, Katie."

The warmth in his voice made her cheeks start to heat. She cleared her throat. "What did Mrs. McKinney say? Anything helpful?"

"Yes. I think we may have something to work with."

Not what she'd expected to hear. She sat a little straighter. "What?"

"She remembers seeing a car, a gray sedan, parked several doors down. She also remembers seeing the car there every day for about two weeks before your sister disappeared."

"Someone staking the place out," she whispered.

"It's one theory, of course, and that's what I think. I could be wrong, but . . ."

"We need to ask the other neighbors specifically about that vehicle."

"I'm already compiling the list. Get this, though. Mrs. McKinney took a picture of the car."

"What?" Her blood started humming. "Why?"

"Well, it wasn't a picture of the car per se. She was taking pictures of her kid on his skateboard. He'd just gotten the board as a birthday present and was up and down the street showing off while she was snapping pictures."

"And of course she had those pictures in an album somewhere." Excitement tripped through her.

"Of course. The car was fuzzy in a few of them, but she let me take the best one of the lot."

"Take a picture and text it to me, will you?"

"Sure."

New hope sizzled. The car wasn't much, but it might turn into something big. "There wasn't any mention of a strange car in the case file."

"No."

"Right."

Anger filled her. "What were Frank and Danny *doing* while my sister was in the hands of a kidnapper, maybe fighting for her life —" Her voice cracked on the last word and she cleared her throat.

"We'll figure it out."

"We sure will." Resolve hardened and she sent up a silent prayer for God's blessing. *Help me find her, Lord.*

They chatted until she reached the hotel. "Cort's waiting on me, just like you said. Parked right outside my room."

"Good. Sleep tight, Kate."

"Bye, Jordan."

Katie hung up and let a smile linger on her lips. She climbed out of her car and was greeted by Cort. "Glad to see you looking good. Sorry about the night of the fire."

She patted his arm. "Don't you worry about that. I appreciate your willingness to do this."

"I miss the job. Being retired ain't all it's cracked up to be."

Katie bid him good-night and entered her room. The text from Jordan came through and she clicked on the picture. A young boy, about twelve years old, looked like he was having a blast as he rolled down the street on his skateboard, arms wide to help with balance.

The screen was small so she couldn't get much detail on the car behind him, but zooming in helped. And she had a picture she could show when they questioned more neighbors about seeing the vehicle. *Thank You, God, for this small step.* Her adrenaline ebbed and exhaustion swamped her.

As she prepared for bed, her stomach rumbled. She'd forgotten to eat. A glance at the clock said she was going to bed at 5:49 p.m. So what? She was exhausted.

She shut the light off and within minutes was asleep.

Jordan inhaled the scent of home-cooked food. Fried chicken and macaroni and cheese. His stomach rumbled. He would be forever grateful that Erica and Max often took pity on him and invited him to share their meals.

He was disappointed Katie had backed out, although he had to admit he was surprised she'd lasted as long as she had. Her body had taken a beating over the last couple of days and was bound to give out before much longer.

Brandon walked into the den, grabbed a

red-and-green Christmas pillow from the seat and flopped onto the couch. Erica's brother had become almost a permanent fixture around the place. So much so that Jordan thought Max might be a little worried about what was going to happen after his and Erica's wedding in a little less than three weeks — on New Year's Day. He couldn't believe Christmas and the wedding were coming up so fast.

Brandon asked, "When are we eating? I'm hungry."

Max laughed. "You're always hungry." He looked at Jordan and sobered. "So, how's it going with Katie these days? I know she was avoiding you for a while there. How's it going now that you two are working together?"

Jordan grunted and set his tea on the coaster. He settled onto the couch. "It's going much better now, but you're right when you say Katie wasn't happy Erica assigned the case to me."

"I know. Strange. Do you know why she was perturbed you got the case?"

"Yes." He didn't say any more.

Brandon and Max exchanged a look. Brandon shrugged and Max rolled the glass between his hands, then said, "I think it's because she's attracted to you."

Brandon snorted.

Jordan jerked then choked a laugh. "What?"

Max shrugged. "That's Erica's deduction."

Jordan lifted the glass of tea to his suddenly dry mouth. He knew she was attracted to him. The feeling was mutual. But that wasn't the reason she hadn't wanted him on the case. "She said something to Erica?"

"Nope. Not a word."

He hadn't thought she would. Then again, she and Erica were tight, so . . . "Oh."

"But women notice these things, you know?"

"Especially Erica," Brandon said, his lips curving into a sardonic smile. "Now that she's found the love of her life, she's determined everyone in her path will do the same."

Max grinned. "Poor Brandon. And yet you keep coming over and giving her opportunities to set you up with her friends."

Brandon patted his trim belly. "If she wasn't such a good cook, you wouldn't see as much of me."

Jordan knew that wasn't true. The man was crazy about his niece, Molly, and was very protective of his sister. When she'd almost been killed by the woman who'd kidnapped her daughter, Brandon and Erica had grown even closer, watching out for one another and pulling together as siblings often did when a crisis hit a family. He looked at Jordan. "But if Erica says she's attracted to you, she is."

"Maybe." He wasn't going to debate his romantic life. Or the lack of. He glanced at his watch and wished they'd get onto another subject. Katie was fine, safely in her hotel room and most likely sound asleep. And he wanted to hurry up with the dinner and discussion and get back to her. In fact, if his invitation to dinner hadn't felt more like a business invitation over a personal one, he'd just go ahead and leave.

But Erica wanted to talk about the case, and Jordan appreciated her willingness to feed him a home-cooked dinner while she did it.

Max pulled at his lower lip. "I hate that Katie didn't feel like coming, but she probably needs the rest more than she needs the food."

"She's definitely had a few long days."

"Max, are you two ready to eat?" Erica asked from the door. Molly stood behind her, flour streaks covering her face and clothes. Jordan's gut clenched like it did every time he was around small children. It wasn't that he didn't like them — he did. They just brought back bad memories. Memories he fought off on a daily basis. Memories he kept at bay most of the time by avoidance. He found working himself to death was better than alcohol. He had enough issues and didn't need to add to his troubles by becoming a drunk.

And prayer. Sometimes prayer helped, too.

He tuned back in as Max said, "We're more than ready. Bring it on." Max stood and Jordan followed him into the kitchen.

He hated that Katie wasn't there, either. He missed her presence. How odd. He shot a text to Cort.

How is she?

Cort responded,

Fine. Sleeping, I think. Lights have been off for about half an hour now. Quiet.

Great. Keep me updated.

Will do.

Jordan put his phone away and bowed his head as Max led the blessing.

Erica looked up after Max said "Amen,"

and said, "Fill me in on Lucy Randall's case and the progress you've made, will you?"

Max choked on his laughter. "Let the man eat, Erica."

She flushed. "Sorry."

Jordan cleared his throat and dug in. While Max and Erica discussed whether or not Erica should hire another person for the Finding the Lost agency, he could feel Molly watching him. When he looked up, he saw her slide Nellie a green bean. The dog ate it.

When Molly realized she'd been caught, her gaze flew to her mother and then to Max, then back to Jordan. She lifted a finger to her lips, and Jordan couldn't help it. He bit back a smile and gave her a slow nod. No way would he rat her out.

Her eyes sparkled with mirth, and she happily plopped a bean in her own mouth. The knot in his belly eased, and he breathed a sigh of relief. Maybe the past could fade after all.

"Don't you think, Jordan?"

Erica's question made him blink. "Huh?"

"You weren't listening to a word we said, were you?"

"Ah, no, sorry. I was . . . um . . . thinking."

Erica narrowed her eyes. "I'm sure I can

guess what you were thinking about."

Jordan felt a flush start to creep up the back of his neck. "Hmm. I won't argue with a woman who feeds me."

Erica laughed and backed off. Jordan enjoyed the food and the company, and even some of the teasing, but he was ready to get down to business. Erica seemed to sense his restlessness and said, "Max, why don't you and Jordan take your coffee into the den. I'll get Molly settled and be there shortly."

Max stood. "Why don't I get Molly settled and you and Jordan can start talking?"

"Guess that's my cue to shove off," Brandon said. He looked at Jordan. "I'll see you later."

Jordan nodded.

"Don't forget, we're having Christmas dinner here," Erica said.

Brandon frowned. "Right. I may have to work. We'll see." He left and Erica sighed then stood and gave Max a smile that made Jordan ache to have someone look at him that way. No, not someone. Katie.

He swallowed hard and followed Erica into the den. The coffee warmed his hands.

"So tell me the latest. What have you learned from Mrs. McKinney?"

■ ■ ■ ■

Katie sat up and looked at the clock. She'd been asleep for an hour and fifteen minutes. Now her nerves hummed and her senses spun. Knowing it would be a futile effort to try to go back to sleep, she tossed aside the covers and turned on the light.

She wanted her house back.

She wanted whoever was trying to kill her behind bars.

She wanted to find her sister.

She wanted a relationship with Jordan.

That last admission wasn't easy, but it was one she couldn't deny.

And she wanted her mother to love her. It seemed that no matter what she did or how hard she tried, it was never good enough.

Tears threatened at the thought, and she pushed them back. She couldn't dwell on that or she'd go nuts. For the next fifteen minutes, she paced the room. Then picked up the phone and dialed her parents' number.

Her mother answered on the second ring. "Hello."

"Hi, Mom."

"How are you, Katie?"

She swallowed. "I'm doing okay. I wanted

to let you know that I hired a maid service to come clean your house for you next week."

Silence echoed for a brief moment, then her mother said, "Well, that's very nice. Thank you."

"Sure." Katie took a deep breath. "I was wondering if you'd like to meet for breakfast one day soon. I'm working a rather complicated case right now, but —"

"I don't think I'll feel up to that, Katie, but thank you for the invitation." The oh so proper politeness made Katie want to weep.

"Okay, well, maybe another time. Is Dad around?"

"Hold on."

Katie bit her lip. She almost wished her mother would yell at her. Anything would be preferable to the cold, polite attitude.

"Hello?"

"Hi, Dad."

"Hi, sweetie."

"She's not warming up at all, is she?"

His sigh echoed. "I'm working on her. At least she's speaking to you."

"True." It was only in the last few years that her mother had climbed far enough out of her depression to even interact with Katie. And every once in a while Katie thought she caught a glimpse of longing and love in her mother's eyes. But before she could act on it, her mother shut it off and shut her out.

It broke her heart. "I'm doing everything I can to make her love me, Dad. What else can I do?" Her voice cracked on the last word and she wanted to call the words back. "Never mind. You don't have to answer that."

"Katie —" His voice wobbled and he cleared his throat. "Your mother loves you, honey. She loves you so much."

"No, I don't think she does," she whispered. "I think she hates me."

"Oh, baby . . ."

"I'm sorry, Dad, I shouldn't have brought it up. Forget it." She took a deep breath. With an effort, she shoved aside the hurt, wondering if she'd ever get used to it. "Dad, I need to ask you something and I want a straight answer."

"What's that?"

"You asked me to drop Lucy's case."

"Yes." She heard his wariness, but appreciated he didn't push the subject of her mother.

"Why?" He sighed and didn't answer. "Dad?" Katie prompted.

"Because it's dangerous," he blurted. "I don't want anything to happen to you.

Please, Katie, don't put yourself in any more danger."

Katie sat stunned. Hearing the worry in his voice nearly undid her as much as her mother's coolness.

"How do you know I'm in danger?"

"Landing in the hospital isn't enough? That fire was deliberately set. The police officer I talked to said you were shot at. You need to stop looking for Lucy."

"Dad, I don't even know that the fire or anything else going on is related to looking for Lucy." She suspected it, of course, but had no real evidence of it.

"Well, I do," he snapped.

Katie paused. "You do? How?"

A heavy sigh filtered through the line. "I . . ."

"You what? Tell me."

"I got a phone call. Someone with a low voice told me to warn you to stop looking for Lucy — or he'd make sure I had another daughter disappear."

Katie sat frozen. Shock raced through her. "When was this?"

"Right after the fire."

"That's why you came to the hospital. To tell me to stop looking for Lucy."

"Yes." She closed her eyes at his husky admission.

"Why didn't you tell me about the phone call?"

"He said not to. Said he'd come after your mom and me if I said he called, so you can't say anything."

As she absorbed the shock that someone related to Lucy's kidnapping had contacted her parents, she said, "He probably didn't want me to try and trace the call."

"Katie, please, drop it. Lucy's gone. It's not worth your life."

"Dad, this is the whole reason I became a detective." She paused. "If I stop looking for her, he wins," she whispered. And her mother would never forgive her. She had to find Lucy. "You really want that?"

"Of course not," he snapped. Katie bit her lip and waited. He finally said in a softer tone, "Of course I don't want him to win, but honey, I can't lose you, too."

Heart in her throat, Katie finished the call with her father with promises to be careful. For a moment she sat there, marveling. Her father loved her enough that he didn't want her looking for Lucy if it put her in danger. She swallowed hard at the realization and wished her mother felt the same way.

Clamping down on her emotions, she called Gregory and filled him in. "Will you try and trace the call and see if the officers on duty in that area will ride by my parents' house more often?"

"Sure."

"Thanks."

Phone calls finished, her mind in a jumble of thoughts, she was debating her next move when her stomach rumbled.

Katie dialed one more number.

"Hello?"

"Do you have any leftovers? I'm starving."

Erica laughed. "Of course. I was just sitting here with Jordan talking about your case. We'd love for you to join us."

In the background, she heard Jordan's low rumble. "Tell her I'll come get her."

Erica started to repeat it, but Katie said, "I heard him. Let me talk to him a minute, please."

She waited while Erica passed the phone to Jordan. "Hey."

"Hey, you don't need to come get me. I'll get Cort to follow me."

He paused. "I suppose that would work. Or you could just let him drive you."

"No. I want my car." She didn't know why she did.

"But Cort's perfectly capable —"

"I want my car, Jordan." He went silent and remorse for snapping at the man who was only trying to help washed over her.

169

"I'm sorry. It's probably a control issue. Everything in my life is out of control. The least I can do is drive myself." She hadn't meant to be quite that blunt. Hadn't even planned on using those words. But there it was. Some subconscious need to be in control had surfaced.

A sigh reached her. "I get it. Just be careful. I'm calling Cort now."

Katie hung up and shrugged on her heavy coat, wincing at the pull in her shoulder and ignoring the various aches and pains she was going to have to live with for a while. She grabbed her weapon and keys and walked out the door.

A light rain fell, and she wondered if it would cause problems on the road. The asphalt didn't feel slick beneath her feet and the temperature hovered just above freezing. She'd be all right.

Katie said, "He wants you to follow me."

Cort waved his phone at her. "I know. No problem."

"You don't have to do this."

"I don't mind." Cort's dark eyes twinkled at her. "You have him wrapped, my girl."

"What are talking about?"

"You two'll figure it out. Now go get in your car in case someone decides to play target practice with your head."

Katie smirked and climbed into her car. She set her phone in the cup holder and waited for Cort to pull behind her.

With his headlights in her rearview mirror, she made her way out of the parking lot and turned left, staying in the right-hand lane. Cort pulled in behind her. Regret filled her that her search for Lucy had caused such disruption in so many lives. She flexed her fingers around the steering wheel and clicked her blinker to turn right even as she pressed the brake to slow for the approaching light.

A car flashed past her then slowed. Her stomach clenched into a knot. She gripped the wheel tightly and kept her eyes on the guy. His brake lights winked at her just before she pulled up beside him.

She turned right on red. Cort's headlights disappeared for a brief moment, then were there again. Her phone rang. She glanced at the number on her caller ID. Jordan.

Katie grabbed the phone. "Hello."

"Just checking on you."

"I'm fine."

"Where are you?"

"Holcombe Street. I'll be there in about ten minutes."

"All right. Cort still behind you?"

She checked the mirror. Bright lights

behind her about two car lengths back. "Right behind me."

"Be careful, Katie."

"I am. I'm going to check in with Gregory and get the latest on Mr. Young. I'll see you in a bit."

He hung up and she bit her lip. Her heart was doing things it shouldn't be doing. Not for him. Jordan Gray was off-limits, but she couldn't seem to keep her distance. He was exactly the kind of man she wanted. And his parents would probably never be able to accept her.

And that was a big enough obstacle for her to put the brakes on her emotions. Shut them up tight and throw away the key.

Or at least try.

Jordan's phone rang. Cort. "What's up?"

"I lost her."

"What? I just talked to her. She said you were right behind her."

"I got cut off when she turned right on Holcombe. Some dude cut in front of me. By the time I got around him, she was gone. Which route would she take, left or right at Henry?"

Jordan thought but didn't know. "I have no idea which way she'd go. Let me call her and ask her where she is."

172

He hung up and punched in Katie's number.

Then groaned when it went to voice mail.

Ten

Katie ignored Jordan beeping in as she talked with her roommate on the phone.

"Unfortunately, I don't have a lot to tell you on Mr. Young. He had no defensive wounds, so he trusted whoever he let in his house. And that person took him by surprise and shot him execution style. He was killed sitting in his chair," Mariah told her.

"Yes, I knew that. Do you have a time of death?"

"You said the house was cold when you entered due to the open doors, and that messes up my timeline. As best I can determine, he died the day of the wreck, but I can't be a hundred percent sure. The shooting at the diner happened at one-oh-four p.m. He was at the hospital for a good wait."

"His neighbor saw him come home with his son. That was around five-thirty p.m."

"As far as I can tell, he was killed shortly after that."

"The killer was waiting for him," she whispered. "But how did he get his information? How would the killer have known who it was?"

"Maybe he got the license plate and got someone to figure it out."

"Or maybe when he raced off and lost the police chasing him, he circled back and watched everything."

"And followed the man to the hospital."

"And then home."

"It could've happened that way."

"Maybe." Katie heard her phone beep again. "I've got to go. Thanks."

"See ya."

She glanced at the screen of her phone. Jordan. She'd missed him again. She smiled. It felt rather nice to have someone worry about her.

Then she frowned. She just wished he didn't have a reason to. She'd call him back as soon as she got on the straight road. He could wait sixty seconds.

Katie turned off the main highway and took the road that would lead her to Erica's home. Erica and Max had bought the property three months ago, shortly after they'd found Molly and brought her home. Max and Erica's wedding was in a few weeks, and Katie couldn't be happier for her friends.

Max had decided to give his house to his sister, Lydia, whom he'd bought it for, anyway. Katie knew he was anxious for the wedding so he could move into the new place and he, Erica and Molly could be a family at last. She started to dial Jordan's number when she noticed the lights behind her.

Cort seemed to be following a little too close. She tapped her brakes. The road was getting slick, and he needed to back off a little.

Cars passed her on the left going in the opposite direction. Streetlights were sparse and the darkness pressed in on her. She shivered and sent up a prayer for safety.

Cort backed off for a few minutes, then he was right back on her tail. What was he doing? Was he trying to get her attention?

She cleared the screen of Jordan's number and started to punch in Cort's when the device rang. Jordan. "Hello."

"Katie, Cort got cut off and lost you. Do you have anyone behind you?"

A frisson of fear shot up her spine. Along with a surge of anger. "Yes, and he's riding my bumper."

"Tell me where you are and I'll call for backup."

"I'm on —"

The car slammed into her bumper and she lost her grip on the phone. It flew to the floorboard. "I'm on Sunset!" She prayed the phone was still on. She didn't dare lean over to retrieve it.

Katie tightened her grip on the steering wheel as she glanced in her rearview mirror and tried to get a look at the face of the person following her. This was not happening again. Hadn't her attacker learned his lesson the first time?

Apparently not.

Under one of the few street lamps, she caught a glimpse of the car. A late-model silver Mustang. It hung back and she slowed.

The Mustang slowed more.

Katie kept her foot on the brake and with her right hand made sure she could reach her weapon easily. She didn't want to remove it from the back of her waistband lest it end up like her phone.

She slowed until she was going twenty miles per hour. The Mustang stayed back. Then shot forward. Katie pressed the gas and the Mustang fell behind.

"Why are you playing with me? Who are you?" she whispered to the image in her mirror. Headlights approached and the car zipped past on her left. Still she kept her eyes on the Mustang.

Icy patches had formed on the road. With the additional rain and now below-freezing temperatures, the roads could be dangerous. She'd worked in this kind of weather for years and driving in it had ceased to bother her. Crime didn't care what the weather was like, and she'd had to learn fast how to drive on the slick roads. However, she'd never had someone trying to kill her while she navigated them.

Katie sped up again, praying she wouldn't hit a sheet of black ice.

The Mustang stayed right with her. Close enough not to lose her and far enough back not to be identified. Not that she would be able to see anything in this darkness.

She shivered as the cool evening air blew through her cracked window. She couldn't afford for the windows to fog up, so she'd lowered it slightly. December in the South. One year it would be in the eighties, the next, freezing. Apparently this was the year for the cold. She loved it.

What she didn't love was someone following her. Being a potential threat. The headlights fell farther and farther behind. Had he given up?

Keeping her eyes on the rearview mirror,

she took the turn that would take her to Erica's house. Trees bordered her right and lined her left. Pastureland stretched behind a white picket fence.

Secluded. Peaceful. Serene.

Longing filled her. What would it be like to find that one person she would feel comfortable enough with to share her life?

Jordan immediately popped into the forefront of her mind. Handsome, strong, quiet. Mysterious. A man with a past. A man that made her blood hum a little faster, and her heart twist with something she refused to acknowledge. Her jaw firmed. *Stop thinking those kinds of thoughts. That's not your life.*

She obeyed the mental order and pondered the strangeness of the Mustang, watching for it, wondering if she should turn around and go after it. She thought about stopping and retrieving her cell phone, but that would leave her vulnerable should her attacker still be back there.

Which he was.

Headlights zoomed up behind her. She pressed the gas pedal. And still they came closer. Katie took a deep breath, pictured the twists and curves to the road ahead of her. She came up with a plan just as the car behind her rammed into her once again.

She jerked into the seat belt, tightened her

fingers around the wheel and brought forth all of the defensive driving techniques she'd ever learned.

Katie slammed on the brakes and spun the wheel to the left. The vehicle came at her again and this time caught her on the driver's side. She kept control, stayed on the road.

Until she hit the patch of black ice that sent her spinning, crashing toward the trees lining the side of the road. The seat belt tightened; her head hit the window. Her car bounced off the first tree, careened into the second and came to a stop, nose down, against the third.

Blackness threatened, her head throbbed. Nausea churned.

Don't pass out, don't pass out.

Katie took a deep breath, fought off the dizziness and encroaching darkness.

Get out of the car. Now. Now.

Night had fallen. A light drizzle dampened her broken windshield. Katie unhooked the seat belt and caught herself on the steering wheel. She pushed against the driver's door with no results.

Stuck. She'd have to get out the passenger side.

With effort, ignoring the throbbing in her head and the nausea churning in her gut, she released the seat belt. She gave a quick glance in the rearview mirror. Saw the headlights at the top of the gently sloping hill.

A shadow outlined by the lights.

A shadow headed her way.

Jordan paced the length of Erica's den. "Where is she? She was getting ready to tell me where she was and I got cut off. Why isn't she answering her phone?" Max came in and Jordan filled him in. "I'm going to look for her."

"I'll go with you."

Jordan slipped into his jacket and followed Max out the door into the frigid, wet weather. The foreboding in his gut bothered him and he offered up a short prayer for Katie's safety.

ELEVEN

With a grunt, Katie shifted. Ignoring her shoulder's screaming protests, she'd managed to crawl over the armrest into the passenger seat and shove open the door. Her cell phone. Where was it? She turned back to the car and searched the passenger-side floorboard. Nothing. She glanced up. The shadow had disappeared. Her eyes darted from one side of the car to the other. Through the windows and behind her.

Where had he gone?

Leaves crunched, and she froze. Looking up, through the driver's window, she could see his head and shoulders, moving closer, slowly, as though he was hesitant to approach the car but compelled to do so.

Katie's stomach lurched and she swallowed hard. The throbbing in her head didn't help the nausea churning her gut. And it felt like the seat belt had left a permanent bruise across her left shoulder, exacerbating the already sore area. Absently, she wondered if she'd pulled her stitches loose. She rolled out of the car onto the frozen ground and bit her lip as pain raced through her.

The cold felt good at first, reviving her a bit, clearing her mind. Then the rain came harder, slithering under her collar, leaving a freezing streak down her back.

Cold seeped through her coat and into her bones.

Her teeth began to chatter as shivers wracked her. She kept an eye on the figure, listened to his footsteps as he crept closer. She wrapped stiff fingers around her weapon and then released it. She wasn't sure she'd be able to pull the trigger. And didn't want to. Yet. Not until she knew who the man was.

She slipped her right hand into her left armpit, desperate to warm her fingers. Shudders racked her. Shock, cold, adrenaline and fear. A combination that sent her body into a tailspin. Trying to control her shakes, she took another look through the window.

The man coming toward the vehicle was not her friend. He was not here to help her. She knew he was the reason her car now kissed the tree. Katie inched her way toward a large tree trunk.

If she hadn't been wounded and nearly frozen stiff, she would have been tempted to pull her weapon and confront him once her fingers warmed up. But right now she felt like fleeing and hiding were her best options.

Decision made, she scooted faster toward the tree. She worried the headlights would illuminate her like they did the man coming after her if she stood. Through the passenger window, she could see the shadow's head and shoulders. Familiarity tugged at her. There was something about his silhouette, like she should know him. . . .

Ribs protesting, head throbbing, shoulder hollering, she kept her lips clamped against any escaping sound. The pain raged through her, but she figured pain was better than death.

And she had no doubt the man who'd run her off the road didn't plan to leave her alive. He was taking his time to investigate the car. Taking the time to make sure she was dead.

She reached the tree and shifted herself behind it. A curse reached her ears, and she clenched her teeth together to keep them from chattering. He'd just realized she wasn't in the car. Shivers racked her. Shock and cold. A deadly combination. But she'd be all right as long as she stayed conscious.

Katie peeked around the tree. Her attacker stood still, his head swiveling from side to side, as though undecided which way to search first. A hard fist slammed against the roof of the car and she flinched.

"Where are you? You're dead, Katie. It's time to give it up. Show yourself and I'll make it quick." The harsh, guttural growl sparked more fear in her belly as reality and disbelief hit her. Having her house burn down around her had been horrifying and scary, but to have him come after her face-to-face with the full intent to kill her without hesitation . . .

That was just plain terrifying.

Jordan peered into the darkness, his head aching with the strain of trying to see. "You're sure this is the route she would take to get to your house?"

Max said, "It's the only route."

Jordan supposed that was good. "What if she wasn't headed over to your house? What if she changed her mind? What if —" He clamped his mouth shut. No sense in what-ifs.

Max said, "It's possible, but I don't know what else to do except —"

"There. Headlights."

"Yeah. Pointed into the woods."

Max accelerated and flashed his lights at the vehicle. A figure darted through the beams and jumped into the car. Tires spun on the slick asphalt, but caught and sped away. Soon the vehicle's taillights disappeared from sight. "I don't like that," Jordan muttered.

"What kind of car, could you tell?"

"No, it's too dark. This road needs some street lamps."

"Let's check out what that guy was in such a hurry to get away from." Max pulled near to where the other car had been parked and pointed his lights into the wooded area. "This is only about a mile from my house. I've got a flashlight in the glove compartment."

Jordan had the flashlight and his door open before Max put the car in park. His feet hit the asphalt as a car approached, then slowed and pulled to the side. Jordan and Max exchanged glances. Jordan got a good look at the vehicle. "Cort," he told Max.

Cort burst from the car, eyes frantic and furious. "Where is she?"

"That's what we're trying to figure out." Jordan swung the high-powered beam around. "Look at that tree." He pointed to a tree with limbs and bark torn off. "Something hit it pretty hard." He started down the hill. "Katie? Katie, are you down there?"

He waved the light and noticed a rough path that had been cut by something heavy. The rain picked up speed, and the cold seeped through his heavy coat. He ignored it, his only concern for Katie.

"Katie?" Max added his voice from the top of the hill. No response. He called, "I'm going to call Gregory and see if he's had any luck."

Jordan moved farther down the hill and his light bounced off metal. "Get down here, Max, Cort. I found her car."

Within seconds, they stood beside him. Max held a second flashlight in his left hand. They made their way to the vehicle. Jordan felt his heart shudder at the sight. "That doesn't look good."

"Is she in there?"

Jordan flashed the beam on the interior. "No. But I see blood." *Lord, let her be okay, please.* "Katie?"

A low groan reached his ears. He paused. "You hear that?"

"Yeah. Back there." Max aimed his light toward the trees on the other side of the vehicle. Jordan stomped through the soggy leaves and underbrush toward a large tree. Another sound.

He rounded the tree. And there she was.

Pale as death.

Katie was cold. So cold. She'd never been so cold in her life. She groaned and reached for the blanket she kept at the end of her bed.

"Katie? Katie, wake up."

She tried, she really did. Her eyes wouldn't open, but she felt the sensation of being lifted, cushioned. Movement. Jordan murmuring in her ear.

A prick in her left arm. Warmth. Finally warmth.

"Let's get her to the hospital."

She tried again to open her eyes. This time she managed to pry her eyelids up to half-mast. What had happened?

Memories rushed at her. The man in the Mustang. He'd run her off the road. Or had it been him?

She noted she was in an ambulance. A paramedic hovered over her. "Katie? You with me?"

"Yeah," she croaked.

Relief relaxed the man's features a fraction. Slowly her muscles lost their rigid tenseness. A blood pressure cuff on her left arm tightened and released. Her nose itched. Heavy blankets weighted her down.

And everything hurt. She gasped.

A warm hand covered hers. She slid her eyes to the right. Jordan. "Hey, what are you doing here?" she whispered.

"Thought I'd come along for the ride." The concern in his eyes stirred something within her. She tried to scowl but couldn't stop her heart from doing that little fluttering thing it did every time she thought about the man. Or heard his name. Or smelled his cologne. It was downright annoying. She did not want to be attracted to him. It would only lead to a broken heart.

But she was. And had been since she'd started to really get to know him almost six weeks ago. And now, with his gentle hold on her hand, she felt her heart slipping even further down the slippery slope she'd put it out on.

"Car. Ran me off the road." It was almost too much of an effort to talk. Now that she was warming up, sleepiness invaded her body. Not the sleepiness like the cold where she knew if she went to sleep, she might not wake up. This was different. Comfortable. Welcoming. She drifted.

Jordan's voice jerked her back. "I know. Max and I think we came up on the vehicle."

"He got away."

"Yes. He did."

She sighed. And frowned. She needed to think, to figure out who wanted to see her dead. Why the man's shadow had seemed so familiar. Later. She was so tired. Her eyes drooped.

Katie woke with a start. Her eyes popped open and awareness hit her hard — along with a headache. She ignored the pain and forced her brain to cooperate. Someone had tried to kill her. Again. Jordan had ridden over in the ambulance and she was in the hospital. Again. This really was getting to be a really bad habit.

And Jordan was now sitting in the chair next to her bed. Snoring softly.

Her heart stirred with an emotion she wasn't sure she could identify, but she found herself blinking back tears. She sighed. Just because he was good-looking and intense didn't mean she had to act like she'd never seen a good-looking and intense man before. She needed to stop thinking about her attraction and worry about who was out to kill her.

She blinked and licked her lips. Dry. She spotted the cup of water with the straw on the tray and tried to reach for it. Sore muscles protested and she couldn't hold back a gasping whimper as pain rippled through her.

Jordan stirred, lifted his head and leaned forward. "Hey, welcome back."

Her heart ignored her lecture of only seconds ago and fluttered at his sleepy concern. "What are you doing here?" He handed her the cup and she took a sip of the cool water.

He smiled. "You already asked me that question." Had she? Oh. Right. In the ambulance. He reached for her hand and squeezed her fingers. "You scared us all to death."

She grunted. "Sorry. Scared myself pretty bad, too. Where are Max and Erica?"

"Keeping all of your cop friends from invading your room and demanding a statement."

She almost smiled but was afraid it would hurt. "And Gregory?"

"Pacing like a caged tiger while he tries to track down who ran you off the road. Last time I talked to him, he had a crime scene unit on the way and a wrecker to pull up your car."

"It's raining — or at least it was. I'll be surprised if they're able to find anything."

"They'll give it a try. I called your insurance company. I'll be surprised if they don't total the vehicle."

"Lovely," she murmured and grimaced at the thought of dealing with everything that awaited her when she was released from the hospital. Again.

A knock on the door interrupted them. Jordan stood and went to open it while Katie closed her eyes and wondered why Jordan was allowing himself to care when he knew as well as she did that they didn't have a chance of working out romantically. But he did care. She could see it in his eyes. More tears surfaced because she was going to have to put the brakes on her emotions, the feelings that were rapidly developing for this man.

Because she just wasn't up to a broken heart.

TWELVE

Jordan frowned and gazed at the crowd still in the waiting room.

He'd answered several questions from Gregory, who looked annoyed with Jordan for asserting himself as Katie's protector. But he frankly didn't care.

Jordan didn't understand his need to be with Katie, but the thought of losing her last night had done something to his heart that he couldn't explain and wasn't sure he even wanted to try. He just knew he'd never felt this way about anyone before and wasn't going to let it slip through his fingers without putting up a good fight for it.

Which was why he'd planted himself in her room: to make sure she wasn't bothered by anyone she didn't want to see. To check and double-check that she was going to be all right.

She needed her rest, not the hounding of her detective friends. And so he'd appointed himself her guardian. Her protector. And so far she'd let him step into that role.

However, he knew she needed to give a statement. He motioned to the detective and Gregory shot to his feet. Within seconds, they were back in her room. She had her eyes closed, her head tucked against the pillow. The pale cast to her skin said she was getting close to being wiped out.

"Don't be long," he said to Gregory.

Gregory grunted, and Katie opened her eyes. She gave a wan smile to her partner. "Glad to see you."

"Not as glad as I am to see you. Twice in one week? You keep landing in this place, they're going to put your name on a room."

She grimaced. "I'm going to hear jokes about this for a long time to come, aren't I?"

"Since you're going to live, yeah."

She gave a little laugh and grimaced. "I figured."

"Don't worry, something will happen to take the heat off you in a couple of months."

Katie gave a pained laugh and a low groan. "Stop making me laugh, it hurts."

Gregory pulled out a green notebook. "I need a statement."

"Someone tried to kill me again. How's that?"

Gregory pursed his lips then said, "It's a start." He flipped to a blank page. "So what are the details?"

"Nothing. I was on that little road that leads to Erica's house. I was driving slow, being careful of the possibility of black ice, thinking Cort was behind me. Then Jordan called and said he wasn't. The guy rammed me, and I dropped my phone." Jordan handed her cell to her.

She placed it on the bed beside her. "Thanks. Headlights came up behind me, and I sped up. The car behind me did, too, and rammed me again. I hit a couple of trees and managed not to die."

She kept her tone light, but Jordan could see the thread of tension in her jaw. A muscle began to tic. She rubbed her hands down the sheet covering her legs. "He got out of the car and came looking for me. I managed to crawl out the other side of the vehicle, facing away from him. When he realized I wasn't in the car, he was mad."

Gregory's gaze turned serious. "He's been after you. He arranged to have Cort cut off so he could follow you without interruption."

"Yeah." She paused. "So does that mean there are two of them after me?"

"Definitely someone who has help. You

think the guy who ran you off the road had something to do with Bobby Young's murder?"

"I don't know, Gregory. I really don't know. Probably. Everything seems tied together." She gave a hard smile. "But that's good. That means we're getting closer. It means someone's nervous."

"So you think this has something to do with your sister's case?" Gregory asked.

"Yes. Definitely," she said.

Gregory raised a brow. "You're still chasing that?"

Katie eyed him, steel in her gaze. "You know I am." She would never have been able to keep that a secret from him. And she hadn't tried. Had no reason to. Gregory understood her need to find Lucy and had even offered to help if she wanted.

He nodded. "Let's just assume that this doesn't have anything to do with Lucy. Is there anything new you've been digging around in? Anything out of the ordinary?"

Katie's eyes shot to Jordan's. "No. I've been thinking along those lines, too. The only thing I've done different is hiring Finding the Lost and getting them involved."

"Then maybe that's the answer," Gregory said. He looked at Jordan. "Someone is nervous about the questions you've been asking. Looks like you've kicked over a bee-hive."

"Looks like," Jordan murmured.

Another knock on the door caught their attention. Jordan opened it, and Erica and Molly stepped inside. Erica rushed over. "Are you all right? I tried to see you earlier, but you were still out cold. Max and Jordan have been keeping me updated."

Molly moved close enough to lean against the edge of the bed. "Aunt Katie, are you gonna die?"

Erica flushed and clapped a hand over the seven-year-old's mouth. She shot an apologetic look at Katie. "No filters, as you know very well."

Katie grinned, grateful for the light-hearted moment in the midst of the thick tension. "I'm not going to die. At least not today. I'm very glad you came to see me, though."

"Me, too. And guess what?"

"What?"

"I'm getting another puppy. A friend for Nellie, only this one's gonna be a baby dog. And I get to walk him and feed him and give him a bath whether he wants it or not, and —"

"All right, kiddo," Erica interrupted. "The puppy's not a done deal, remember?"

The little girl's face dropped, and Katie wanted to hug her. "I'll talk to her," she whispered.

Molly's face lit up, and she shot a triumphant look at her mother, who in turn sent Katie an exasperated frown. Katie shrugged and a pang hit her as she realized her interaction with Erica was one she might have had with Lucy had her sister not disappeared. She blinked away the sudden moisture and tapped Molly's nose. Composed once again, she looked up at Erica, whose eyes had turned serious.

She said, "This hospital thing is starting to be a habit with you."

Katie grimaced. "So I've been told. Don't worry, I plan on breaking it, and fast." She knew she would be sore and achy for a couple of days. She supposed she should be used to it by now. A yawn caught her off guard. Embarrassed, she said, "I think my painkillers are catching up with me."

Erica squeezed her hand. "Get some rest. I'm serious, though. I would love for you to come stay with us if you need to."

Katie swallowed. "Thanks, Erica. But —" she shot a glance at Molly "— I'd never put your family in danger." Erica squeezed her hand and Molly gave her a gentle hug.

They left and Jordan said, "You should

take her up on it."

Katie shut her eyes. "You know I can't do that."

"Yeah."

She heard Jordan leave just before sleep claimed her.

Jordan decided to grab a few hours of sleep. The exhaustion pursuing him had finally caught up, and Katie had pushed him to go home and rest. Jordan caved, realizing he wasn't going to be any good for her if he was punchy and less alert than usual. After assessing the security situation, he had agreed he should take advantage of the willingness of others to help and get some sleep.

She had a guard on her door in case the guy who had tried to kill her decided to come back and finish the job. Plus a few of her off-duty police officer buddies milled in the waiting room. Most had gone home, but the ones she was close to remained, determined to watch over one of their own.

It was obvious Katie was well-liked and respected by those she worked with. She was good at her job. She cared and yet managed to keep her sanity. Not everyone did.

When he woke, it was Friday morning. As he dressed, he debated his feelings for Katie.

He remembered the sense of loss he'd felt when he realized Cort wasn't behind her and she was in danger once again.

He swallowed hard. He could have lost her. Almost had. The fact that he was even debating pursuing a romantic relationship with a woman his parents held such animosity for told him he was in way over his head.

And he knew he was going to have to talk to his parents. Tell them the truth about Neil. And not for the first time, he second-guessed himself in withholding the truth from them. Was he being selfish? Allowing them to put their youngest son on a pedestal? He hadn't wanted to tarnish their memories by telling them, but was that the right thing to do?

He grappled with the questions until a headache started to build. He grabbed his keys and headed out the door to climb into his car. He dialed Katie's number at the first red light. "I'm guessing you had a quiet night?" he asked.

"I did. No one was getting in this room with all of my volunteer bodyguards outside. Gregory sent them all home around midnight, then he stayed outside the door the rest of the night."

"Glad to hear it." She sounded better. Stronger. "Have you gotten a clean bill of health yet?"

"Somewhat. Erica's on her way to take me home."

"I was on the way to do that, but I can catch up with you later if you prefer." If she had a ride, he could go by his parents' house.

"Erica's bringing me some clothes and other items, but I appreciate the offer."

"Of course. Do you have an escort?"

"Max. And I think Gregory was going to come, too."

"Good." She should have enough help if someone tried anything. He paused and made a decision. "I've got an errand to run. Should take me about an hour. After that I was going to talk to Mrs. Johnson and see if she remembered anything about a strange car in the neighborhood. I thought if you felt up to it, you could go with me."

"Oh. Okay. Right."

He wondered if she was fidgeting with the sheet like she'd done yesterday when she was uncomfortable. "What's going on, Katie?"

A sigh greeted him. "I'm considering dropping the investigation."

For a moment, he wasn't sure what to say. "Those are the last words I expected to come out of your mouth."

"I know." He pictured her rubbing her forehead. "My father called me again this morning. He keeps trying to convince me to stop investigating. He's really worried. And I'm . . . torn." She blew out a sigh. "It's so odd. I never thought I'd hear him say anything like that. When I became a detective and started looking for Lucy, he was so . . . hopeful. And now —" He heard commotion in the background. She said, "Erica's here."

"All right. I'll meet you at your hotel in thirty minutes. I can run my errand a little later. We'll go see Mrs. Johnson first."

"Okay, sure."

"I'll be right there." He hung up and took the next left. His parents needed to know what had happened to Neil. He didn't want to tell them — in fact he dreaded doing so. But he'd been a coward for long enough. It was time to lay the truth on the table. He wasn't going to let a lie keep him from finding happiness with Katie. He didn't want to hurt his parents or taint their memories of Neil, but if he was ever going to be able to have a relationship with Katie, his parents had to hear the truth. He just had to find the words to do it.

As for Lucy Randall, she was a missing child who would now be an adult if she was still alive. But fourteen years ago, she'd been a child who had lived and breathed, had hopes and dreams. Just like the child Jordan had failed to find, just like the one he'd let die. The emotions that came with the memory came hard and swift and he gasped.

No. He was going to find Lucy. It didn't matter that fourteen years had passed. She needed to be found. She deserved to be given justice. And no matter what Katie said, Jordan was determined to make sure Lucy got what she deserved.

THIRTEEN

Friday, midmorning, Katie stood at the window of her hotel room. Jordan pulled into the space in front of her door, and Cort climbed from his vehicle to greet him. He crossed the parking lot to shake Jordan's hand. Katie stepped outside. "You made good time."

"You look like you've been hit by a truck." His soft-voiced concern dispelled any indignation that might have risen at his words. And he was right. She looked awful.

Cort shot Katie a guilty look. "I guess I'm losing my touch. That's twice now he's gotten to you."

"It's not really your fault. I'm beginning to think this guy is trained and has inside information."

"What do you mean?"

She nodded to her room. "Why don't y'all come in and we'll talk a little before Jordan and I go see Mrs. Johnson."

The men followed her inside and planted themselves at the round table in the corner. "What kind of inside information?" Jordan demanded.

She shook her head. "I don't know. He knew what hotel I was staying in because he was watching for me to leave. He knew Cort was helping me and he had someone working with him to cut Cort off so he could get behind me. And they worked it at just the right moment so I wouldn't know what happened. Sure, it was a gamble as to whether it would work or not, but they tried it. And almost won."

She paced in front of the table. "This guy doesn't have any trouble finding me. He seems to know my every movement. He didn't try to strike at me in the hospital either time — he catches me on the road or in my house, places with no cameras and a good chance for him to get away. And he threatened my parents anonymously."

"He doesn't want to get caught," Cort said.

"Absolutely not."

Katie's phone rang and she ignored her aches and pains as she moved to get it from her purse. "Hello?"

"Hey, it's Mariah. Are you okay?"

"Yes, I'm fine." She paused. "Well, I'm

still alive, so I suppose that qualifies as okay."

"I'm sorry I haven't been around. I've been working almost nonstop over the last few days and taking care of Grandma Jean in the interim."

"Don't worry about it. It's probably safer for you not to be around me right now."

Mariah blew a raspberry. "I'd help fight back, you know that."

Katie smiled. She appreciated her friend's willingness to fight on her behalf. "Well, the lab is much safer. Speaking of . . ."

"Right." Mariah turned all business. "Your guy got a little careless. I just got my hit from IAFIS and we have a fingerprint from your Molotov cocktail bottle."

"Who does it belong to?" Her stomach tightened in anticipation of hearing the name of the person who wanted her dead.

"He's a parolee. His name is Norman Rhames."

"Norman Rhames!"

"I take it you've heard of him?"

"Yes. I have. He's the guy who made that deposit into Lisa West's bank account. Her husband is the one who killed the guy who broke into my house."

"Never a dull moment for you, is there?"

"You're funny. But no, never a dull moment." She bit her lip. "Okay, this is an interesting twist."

"Well, I hope you find him. That's my home, too, and I want this guy stopped." Fury seeped through her words and Katie empathized.

"Thanks for the information. I'll pass it along to Gregory and let him work with it. I'm chasing another lead. Maybe one of us will come up with something."

"Sounds good."

"How's Grandma Jean and her cold?"

"She's better and so far I haven't gotten it." Mariah paused. "Of course, I've only been there to sleep at night. I've hardly been around her. My poor mother is not faring so well, I'm afraid."

"Glad she's better. And I'll say a prayer for your mom." Katie blew out a sigh. "I'll let you know what happens with Mr. Rhames."

"Be careful, Katie."

"Yes, ma'am."

She hung up and passed on the information to Jordan and Cort, then called Gregory and filled him in.

"I'll track him down ASAP," Gregory said. "I'll call you as soon as he's in custody."

Katie said, "Please do. I have a few questions for him." Like why someone who deposited five thousand dollars in the account of the wife of a felon was the same person who tried to kill her the other night.

"I'm sure. Are you all right? Need a hand with anything?"

"No, but I appreciate everything you've done so far."

Gregory snorted. "Haven't done much."

"You're not complaining about my absence, you're helping me track down information and you're picking up the slack on our cases. I can't tell you how much I appreciate that."

"You'd do the same for me."

"You know it."

"What's on the agenda for today? You going to take it easy, or is that a dumb question?"

"What do you think?"

He laughed. "I figured."

"We're going to talk to Mrs. Johnson at the nursing home. See if she remembers anything about a gray sedan being parked in the neighborhood."

"Be careful, Katie."

"You know it." She hung up, grateful for a partner she trusted and one who supported her efforts in finding Lucy.

Jordan stood. "Thanks for your help, Cort. Having you watching is the reason Katie is alive. If you hadn't been behind her and called . . ." He shrugged.

Cort shook hands with Jordan and gave a disgusted snort. "If I had been a little quicker with the steering wheel, I wouldn't have lost her."

Jordan turned to Katie and said, "Do you feel up to visiting Mrs. Johnson now?"

"I'm sore, of course, but yes, I'm up to it."

"Do you mind if I drive?"

She gave a low chuckle. "Unless you want to hitchhike, that's pretty much our only option right now." She sighed. "I guess I need to put car shopping on my list of things to do."

"Are you getting a rental?"

"It should be ready by the time we finish with Mrs. Johnson. Erica lined it all up for me."

"She's a good friend."

"She is."

Cort stood and said, "Guess I'll be going, unless you want me to follow and watch for a tail?"

Jordan nodded. "That'd be great."

They filed back out of the room, and Katie joined Jordan in his car. She clicked on her seat belt. "Have your parents said anything more about us working together?"

The abrupt question didn't faze him. "No. And I haven't exactly gone out of my way to talk to them since the confrontation in the restaurant. I was thinking about that earlier and I've decided I'm going to have to make some time to do that."

His low words had a tightness to them, and she almost regretted bringing the subject up, but she and Jordan were growing closer by the day. And if it wasn't for his parents' hatred of her, she'd encourage the relationship. As it was . . .

"They don't know the whole truth," Jordan said.

"What do you mean?"

"That night you arrested Neil. They don't know everything he was doing that night." He cleared his throat. "I kept it from them."

Katie gaped. "Then I don't know the whole story, either. I thought it was just a DUI. Are you telling me there's more?" She glanced in the rearview mirror and saw no one behind them.

"Yes."

"Do you mind sharing?"

He sighed. "Apparently, Neil was a drug mule."

Katie gasped. "What?"

"When they did the autopsy, they found bags of heroin in his stomach."

"Oh, no."

Jordan's lips twisted. "He'd just gotten back from Mexico. From what I can figure out, you stopped him on his way from the airport to deliver the drugs."

"How did you find all this out?"

He slanted a glance at her. "I have my sources."

"But I smelled alcohol on him. He registered twice the legal alcohol limit on the Breathalyzer."

"I know. I'm not saying he wasn't drinking. In fact, he probably had a few on the plane, as he always hated flying. But there was more to it than that."

Katie blew out a breath. "Wow. And you never told your parents this?"

"No." He pinched the bridge of his nose. "Dad's in his late fifties. But about two years ago, he had a mild heart attack."

"Oh. I'm sorry."

"He seemed to bounce back from it pretty well, but my mother is a worrywart. She keeps telling me we need to spare him as much stress as possible."

"Is she right?"

"I don't know. The day of Neil's funeral, he had another heart attack. This one more severe. So . . ." He shrugged. "I'm sure all the stress didn't help."

"So you kept all of this information to yourself."

"Yes."

"So why tell him now?"

"Like I said, I've been thinking. All of the anger and resentment and bitterness he's harboring toward you surely can't be good for him, either."

"True."

"I think what I'm going to have to do is tell my parents about Neil. It's time."

"What if he has another attack?"

He blew out a heavy sigh. "His last check up was good. No sign of any more damage. He's going to have to face what Neil was into if he's going to have any kind of peace. Right now he's in such denial, he's simply adding stress to his life — and his heart."

Jordan pulled into White Oak Manor's parking lot. He shut off the engine and turned to face her. "This isn't something I just came up with. I've been contemplating it for the last six months."

"I see." She looked at her fingers. "And you've decided now is the time?"

"I think so. I've been praying about it."

"And?"

"I don't know. God hasn't said yes or no in a way that's loud and clear."

"So why do it now?"

"For reasons I've already stated, but I won't deny part of it's because I want to explore whatever is developing between us. And I can't do that as long as my parents are planted firmly in the way."

Katie blinked. Shock zipped through her, followed by surprise and then . . . hope. "What do you think is developing?"

Jordan moved in closer and placed a hand at the base of her neck. "This," he whispered. And covered her lips with his. Warm honey moved through her veins, making her languid and giddy with the thought that she could kiss this man forever. She reached up and cupped his chin as he deepened the kiss, and she wanted to protest when he pulled away with a gentle smile. He gazed down at her. "That. And more." He stroked her cheek. "I've never met anyone like you before, and I want to see if we have something special." He tilted his head. "Correction. I think we do have something special, and I want the freedom to explore just how special it is."

She swallowed hard and let out a breath. "Wow." He wasn't holding anything back right now and his openness, his vulnerability stunned her.

"Exactly."

"Okay."

"Okay what?"

"Talk to your parents if you think that's what you need to do." Then she frowned and tried to ignore the effects of his kiss. With just one kiss, he'd stirred up the longing for a relationship with him, the hope for a possible future together.

She thought for a moment, trying to figure out the best way to say what was in her heart. Finally, she said, "I'll be straight with you, Jordan. As much as I'd also like to see where this could go between us, I don't know if I can do it if your parents hate me." She bit her lip, then said, "In fact, I'm pretty sure I can't." She heard the anguish in her last two words and when he flinched, knew he'd heard it, too.

Jordan and Katie walked into the lobby of the assisted-living home and stopped at the front desk. Katie flashed her badge and asked for Mrs. Johnson's room while Jordan stood by a window and watched the parking lot.

"Who was here?" Katie asked.

Jordan tuned in to the conversation.

The lady behind the desk said, "I think it was her son. He came in and she seemed confused as to who he was. That happens a lot these days, poor dear. She is almost ninety, you know."

"Yes, I know, thanks. Do you think it would be possible for us to just speak to her briefly? I promise we won't keep her long. It's really urgent that I talk to her if she feels up to it."

The woman hesitated then said, "Let me check with her nurse. She was apparently pretty agitated when her son left."

Katie shifted beside him. "She's going to say no."

"Why do you say that?"

"I just have a feeling. Come on."

"Where are we going? We don't have her room number."

"Sure we do. I can read upside down. She was documenting something in the chart and snapped it shut when I walked up, but not before I saw the name and a number I'm guessing is her room."

They made their way down the hall to Mrs. Johnson's room. Jordan held the door for Katie, then slipped in behind her. The dark room held the odor that seemed to be indigenous to nursing homes and hospitals: antiseptic, bleach and air freshener.

"Mrs. Johnson?" Katie's soft voice brought his attention to the woman in the bed. A night-light burned in the corner. "Mrs. Johnson?"

Jordan turned on a small lamp and the low-wattage bulb bathed the room in a soft glow.

The woman on the bed stirred. Katie sat in the chair next to her and took her hand. "Hi, Mrs. Johnson. Do you remember me? Katie Randall?"

Mrs. Johnson blinked owlishly, and Jordan picked up a pair of glasses and slipped them on her nose.

"Oh, Katie," Mrs. Johnson said, her voice paper thin and wispy. "Yes, of course I remember you. Will you help me sit up? I must have dozed off." She clicked her teeth and sighed. "I seem to do that a lot lately."

Katie pressed the button, and soon Jordan heard the bed whirring as it lifted its occupant into a sitting position.

"What are you doing in here?"

Jordan spun to see the woman from the front desk. "We decided to come on back and visit."

"Why didn't you wait on me? Her son asked that she not be disturbed."

"That man wasn't my son."

The nurse hurried in. "Now, Mrs. Johnson, you know you sometimes get confused. Of course that was your son."

"Young lady, I do get confused, but I have never not known my own son. I don't have dementia, and I don't have Alzheimer's, so I would appreciate you not trying to make it sound like I do. I'm old and occasionally forgetful, but that was not my son. Now, please go away and let me enjoy my visitors."

The long speech seemed to wind her, but Jordan saw a twinkle in Mrs. Johnson's eyes. A twinkle that blasted hope through the room. The nurse blew out a breath of exasperation but turned and left the room without another word.

Mrs. Johnson looked at Katie. "Did you ever find your sister?"

Katie blinked. So Mrs. Johnson did remember. Katie had almost decided fourteen years would be too much for the elderly woman. "Do you remember the day she was taken?"

"Like it was yesterday." She snorted and coughed. "Can't remember what I had for breakfast, but I'll never forget that day. If only I hadn't asked you to help me carry in those groceries." A tear leaked down her lined cheek. Katie grabbed a tissue and wiped it away.

"It's not your fault, Mrs. Johnson."

A trembling hand lifted to rub her nose. "Well, sometimes I feel like it was."

Jordan shifted. "We think the man who took Lucy was watching, just waiting for an opportunity. If it hadn't been that day, it would have been another time."

That seemed to settle her. "He was watching?"

Katie said, "We think so. Do you remember seeing a strange car parked on the street a couple of weeks before the day of the kidnapping?"

"A strange car? No, I don't think so." She sniffed. "I remember wondering what that police car was doing out there day in and day out, but that's the only car I remember thinking was strange."

"Police car?"

"Uh-huh. Lucky it was so close that day, wasn't it?"

"Yes, very lucky. Mrs. Johnson?"

"Hmm?"

"Who was the man that came to see you, and why did they think he was your son?"

"Guess he told them he was."

"What did he want?"

Her eyes clouded and drooped. "To tell me to be quiet, but I'll talk if I want." Her words slurred, her eyes closed and a snore slipped out.

Katie's eyes met Jordan's. "I think she's done."

He tapped Mrs. Johnson's shoulder. She snorted and her head lolled over to her left shoulder. Jordan sighed. "I think you're right."

Katie stood and winced as her sore muscles protested. She ignored the pain and made a mental note to take some more ibuprofen. "Why hasn't anyone else said anything about a police car being there?"

They walked from the room together. Jordan shook his head. "There were so many police cars there that day most neighbors probably didn't think anything about it."

"Maybe."

"And maybe the police car wasn't really parked. Maybe it was just doing drive-bys, you know?"

"That's possible, I suppose, but she did say 'parked there day in and day out.' "

"You think it's the same car Mrs. McKinney saw?"

"I don't suppose there's any way to know. Mrs. McKinney didn't identify it as a police car, though. Just a gray sedan. And the picture is too unclear to determine if the vehicle is actually an unmarked car."

"You think the man who came to see Mrs. Johnson was the man after me?"

"I don't see how. He wouldn't know we were coming today."

"Right."

"It does seem strange to me, though, that she would get a visitor telling her to keep quiet."

"Did you tell anyone that we were coming here?"

Katie thought about it. "Just Gregory."

"You don't think that was him at the home, do you?"

She frowned. "No way. He was tracking down Norman Rhames. And besides, why would he do that?"

"I don't know. It's just weird. I think we should get the video footage and see who Mrs. Johnson's visitor was."

Katie nodded. "Good idea." She made the required calls and was promised a return call when she could go see the videos.

Once outside the building, Jordan hovered, placing his arm around her shoulder and tucking her close to his side. While she relished the proximity, his touch set her bumps and bruises to screaming. She eased away from him and he shot her a look with a big question mark in his eyes. "Sorry, it hurts."

Realization dawned and regret flickered. "Stay next to me then." Warmth flickered in her midsection. She liked being close to him, wanted his arm around her. He glanced around. "If someone's going to shoot, I want to make you as small a target as possible."

Laughter burst from her before she could choke it back.

Jordan helped her into the car and shut the door, then climbed in his side. He looked at her. "What in the world are you laughing about?"

"I'm sorry. I was just thinking how I was enjoying being close to you, that it was sweet you wanted me tucked up under your arm and you're just worried about me getting shot." She laughed again until tears formed. She swiped them away. "I think I'm hysterical, because it's really not that funny."

He kissed her. She leaned in and felt her emotions even out. Her tears stopped and she hitched a breath and kissed him back.

When he pulled away, his eyes held soft compassion as well as other emotions she wasn't sure she could identify. He said, "I want you close, Katie."

She bit her lip, then gave him a watery smile. "Good."

"I'm taking you back to your hotel room. You need some rest."

Katie leaned her head back against the seat. Exhaustion swamped her. "I think I won't argue with that."

■ ■ ■ ■

Jordan slept in the car outside her hotel room from 3:00 a.m. to 7:30 a.m. Saturday morning. Gregory had taken the first shift. Jordan's five hours of protection duty gave him time to think. And he'd made a decision. One he had to run past Katie. He texted her.

Sitting outside your room. Ready when you are.

Coming. Slowly.

Sore?

To say the least. Be there in a few min.

Ten minutes later, Katie emerged from her room, and he smiled in sympathy as she climbed into the car with a grimace.

He handed her a mug and poured her a cup of coffee from the Thermos. She took a sip and sighed, a grateful sound that made him glad he could do something for her. "You're my favorite person this morning," she murmured.

He laughed. "Glad I could help you out."

He turned serious and gripped the steering wheel. "I want you to go with me somewhere."

"Where?"

"You know that errand I said I needed to run yesterday?"

"Yes."

"I want you to run it with me."

Wary now, she glanced at him from the corner of her eye. "And where might that be?"

"To talk to my parents. I'm going to tell them what really happened with Neil."

A long pause. She finally said, "I don't think that's a good idea, Jordan. If their reaction at the restaurant is any indication of how they still feel —"

"Please." His fingers tightened on the steering wheel. "It *is* how they feel, and it needs to be addressed. I think they need to see you're not some monster."

"I don't know. They may never speak to you again if you bring me around."

"It's something I think we need to try."

"Jordan, they're hurting. It's only been a year."

"I know, but they're not healing. That's the problem. I understand it's only been a year. I still hurt when I think about him, too, but the anger they still hold toward you . . ." He shook his head. "At the restaurant, you would have thought Neil died two weeks ago, their anger was so fresh and raw. It's not right."

"Exactly. Which is why I don't think it's a good idea for me to go."

"Please." He kept his voice low, his tone convincing. "I've already thought about the safety issue. Max is going to follow us."

"Jordan . . ." She drew his name out and he sensed capitulation.

Jordan took her hand and squeezed her fingers. "I want them to see you as you. Not as the woman they believe killed their son." He drew in a deep breath. "I think they need that as much you do."

She sat still and looked at him. "I'm still not sure it's the best idea, but if it's that important to you, I'll do it."

He lifted her hand to his lips and pressed a kiss to her knuckles. Her eyes met his. "Thanks," he whispered.

She nodded and he dropped her hand. "I've already called them. They're expecting me."

"They're early risers."

"Obscenely early. Mom's already started baking."

As Jordan drove, Katie stayed quiet, lost in her thoughts. He left her alone and silently rehearsed how he wanted to break his news of Neil's drug involvement to his parents. Nothing he came up with sounded right. He had a feeling nothing would.

Jordan pulled into his parents' drive, but didn't cut the motor. From the vehicle behind them, Max waved, indicating they were in the clear. No one had followed. Jordan waved back. For several long minutes he simply sat there, staring at the house he and his brother had grown up in.

"It's nice," Katie said.

The house was a modest two-story cottage-style home. His favorite feature was the wraparound balcony on the second floor. Christmas lights wove in and out of the spindles like kudzu. A white wreath hung on the door and bright-eyed reindeer graced the lawn.

"Yes. I had a great childhood. Ideal, really." He gave a slight smile.

"What are you thinking?"

"That my mother always worried we'd play airplane or try to parachute off that balcony and break our necks."

"But you didn't?"

"No way. I had a pretty good sense of self-preservation." He frowned. "Too bad Neil didn't." Neil had found another way to break his mother's heart.

Jaw clamped against his rising emotions, he pulled all the way into the two-car carport that was enclosed on three sides. He twisted the key and silence fell between them. Jordan opened the car door and climbed out. "Could you wait here for a few minutes?"

Katie slid him a glance from the corner of her eye. "You did tell them I was coming, right? You said you'd already called them, that they were expecting us." He moved to the back of the carport, and Katie climbed out of the car to follow him. "They know, right, Jordan?"

"I said they were expecting me."

Her face lost all color. "You can't spring me on them."

"I know. But I didn't want to tell them over the phone. I couldn't think of a good way to explain it. Could you hang back a little until I tell them?" He glanced around. "And stay down. We weren't followed, but that doesn't mean you're safe."

"That's why you parked in the carport? To give me cover while you broke the news to your parents?" She shot back into the car and slammed the door, glaring daggers at him.

He grimaced and didn't blame her. He'd taken the coward's way out by not telling

226

his parents she was coming with him and not telling Katie he hadn't told his parents. "I'm sorry. You're right. I'm a big coward when it comes to this kind of thing."

Her eyes softened slightly. "I'll just make some phone calls."

"Thanks, Katie."

Jordan went around to the front door and tried the knob. Locked. His lips twisted into a smile in spite of his roiling emotions. Maybe all of his preaching about safety had sunk in. He knocked, and his dad opened the door. Pleasure lit his features. "Jordan, good to see you, son. Come on in."

Jordan entered the small foyer and breathed in the scent of his childhood. Depending on the season, he always knew what his mother's house would smell like: December meant homemade chocolates, pies and cakes. His mouth watered. "I need to talk to you and Mom, but first I'm going to have a taste of whatever she's cooking in there."

His dad grinned at him, and Jordan felt a surge of remorse at the pain he was about to put them through. He studied his father. In his late fifties, Paul could still pass for mid-forties, in spite of his heart issues. Jordan hoped he aged as well — without the heart problems. He shucked his coat and hung it on the rack by the door as he wrestled with the reason he'd come over.

Jordan's mother stood at the oven, placing another pan of goodies on the rack. "Hi, Mom."

"I thought I heard you." She turned and crossed the room to give him a hug and a peck on the cheek. "How are you doing?"

"I'm doing all right."

Jordan snagged a sweet treat from the cooling rack and popped it in his mouth. The sugary concoction melted on his tongue. "Mmm. Delicious as always." He smiled. "I heard you were in your Christmas baking mood. I could smell this stuff all the way from my apartment."

Her eyes twinkled up at him. Jordan noticed time hadn't been quite as kind to her as it had to his father. Fine lines radiated across her forehead and around her mouth and eyes. Grief had added more than her fair share, he supposed.

Anger at Neil surged and he bit his lip. "I need to talk to you and Dad. Do you have a minute to sit down?"

"Sure I do." She pulled off the red-and-white checked apron with the big red heart that said *50 and Fabulous*. He'd given it to her four years ago when she'd bemoaned her fiftieth birthday for six full months. He noticed she wore it every time she worked in the kitchen.

The three of them sat at the kitchen table. Jordan snagged another chocolate, scrambling to find the words he'd practiced on the way over. They'd deserted him.

He took a deep breath and for one frantic moment wondered if he was being selfish. Were his words necessary? Would they do more harm than good? Would his parents even believe him?

Maybe not at first. But eventually they would. And that was when it would hurt the most. When the truth of Neil's actions finally sank in.

"What is it, son?" His dad clapped him on the back.

Jordan rubbed his forehead. "I need to tell you guys something and I'll just tell you straight up, it's not going to be easy for you to hear."

Matching frowns immediately appeared on their faces. His mother covered his hand with hers and her eyes narrowed, searching his expression. "What is it you don't want to tell us?"

She could always read him. Jordan shook his head. "I've been thinking — and praying — long and hard about telling you this, but the fact of the matter is, I don't think you

—" he looked at his father "— most especially you, Dad, are healing from Neil's death."

"Healing?" His father's eyebrows came to a V at the bridge of his nose. "Healing? How are we supposed to heal when the cop who helped kill your brother is out there free to kill other kids?"

Jordan held on to his temper with effort. He hadn't come here to argue with his parents. He knew just mentioning Neil's name was enough to set his dad off on a tangent.

"They did an investigation, Dad, thanks to your insistence. There was nothing to prove she'd been negligent. Neil was drunk. He was arrested for driving under the influence and he was placed in a holding cell. End of story." He clasped his hands between his knees and prayed for wisdom.

"It's not the end! She placed him in a cell with a killer!"

Jordan thought his head might explode with the effort of holding in his temper. "She didn't do anything wrong. Neil was drunk when he chose to drive. He ran a stop sign going fifty miles per hour right in front of Detective Randall. What else was she supposed to do? She did her job. It was Neil's stupid choices that killed him, not her."

His father stood and jabbed a finger at Jordan. "I refuse to sit here and listen to you defend her. I can't believe you would come into my house —"

Jordan slammed his palm onto the table. His father jerked, and his mother gasped. Jordan took a deep breath. "Stop. Okay? Just stop." He looked at his dad. "And sit down, please. I'm not done." His father, still staring at Jordan's uncharacteristic outburst, slid back into his chair.

"Why do you say she didn't kill him?" his mother whispered, her stricken expression zinging straight to his heart.

"Because I know the truth about Neil. Truth I've kept from you, thinking to spare your feelings, your memories." He looked at his dad. "Your heart. But I —"

"What truth?" His father's voice was low, the question, wary.

Katie sat in the car and felt her anger dissipate with each passing moment. She understood Jordan's reluctance to tell his parents over the phone that she was coming along. If Jordan had told his parents he was bringing her by, most likely they would have flipped out. His father would have stewed and stressed over it. She wasn't exactly sure how his mother would have reacted.

She understood Jordan's thinking. When he told his parents she was sitting in the car outside, they might be a little more likely to see her. If only out of good manners.

Although good manners hadn't stopped Jordan's father from heaping his grief and anger on her head in the morgue. Or at the restaurant.

Katie moved the rearview mirror to give her a good view of the area behind her. Max and Jordan seemed confident they hadn't been followed, but Katie wasn't going to relax her guard. She called Gregory, who'd followed up on the receipt they'd found in the shooter's wrecked and abandoned car.

"Are you in or out of the hospital?" he answered by way of a greeting.

Katie grimaced. "Out."

"Try and keep it that way, will you?"

She heard the concern in his voice and appreciated it. "I'll do my best. It's been so crazy, I haven't had a chance to track down that receipt. Did you?"

"I did."

"And?"

"And our shooter had on sunglasses and a ball cap along with a scarf wrapped around his neck."

"Video footage?"

"Yes. But my guess is he was familiar with

the camera placements, because he kept his back to them as much as possible."

"And he paid in cash."

"At the pump. He never entered the store."

"Of course." She sighed and watched the door leading into the house. No sign of Jordan. "So that's another dead end."

"Maybe. I mean, we're looking for a guy who's about five feet eleven or six feet tall. He's a little overweight and is Caucasian. Couldn't get hair or eye color, of course, but this information might help."

"What about his hands? Could you do any close-ups?"

"He was wearing black gloves."

Of course he was. "All right. Thanks. Let me know if you come up with anything else."

"Will do."

She hung up then dialed her mother's number. Voice mail. She left a message about stopping by soon and hoped she was well. Katie avoided mentioning her stay in the hospital and her mother's noticeable absence.

And the hurt that it caused.

She winced and glanced in the mirror. Nothing. Another look at the door to the house. Another nothing. Jordan sure was taking a long time.

Even though it was Saturday, Katie knew Mariah was working. She called her roommate for an update on the diner evidence. Mariah said, "Bullet casings came from a semiautomatic .308 Winchester rifle. It's not a hard weapon to get your hands on, and there's nothing really special about it. Lots of hunters use it."

"Lovely. Anything else?"

"Trace evidence such as hair and other fibers that don't add up to anything right now, but will be available for comparison if you come up with a suspect."

"Okay."

"So what are you doing on your medical leave?"

Katie glanced at the house and caught Jordan's eye, staring at her from behind the window of the kitchen door. "Getting ready to walk into the lion's den, I think."

Jordan met Katie's eyes through the glass and shook his head. He paced back to the table and sat again, wishing he could take out his agitation on the patterned linoleum floor. Instead, he shifted and cleared his throat. "Neil was into drugs. Not just using them, he was a mule." He paused at his parents' blank expressions. "Someone who transports drugs over the border for a lot of money by swallowing packets of drugs."

His mother blinked at him, her audible gasp making Jordan grasp her hand. She pulled away and stared at him as the color in her cheeks drained away.

"How dare you?" His father jumped up, face red, eyes blazing. "She's brainwashed you! How dare you come into this house and malign your brother's memory? How dare you!" He strode from the kitchen.

"Dad —" Jordan moved to follow. His mother's hand on his arm stopped him. Her white, pinched face sent sorrow racing through him. "I'm sorry. I shouldn't have . . ." He shook his head.

"No. It was time."

Her quiet response had him looking into her eyes. "What do you mean?"

She wiped her hand on her apron and clasped them in front of her. "About six months before Neil died, I heard him being sick in the bathroom. I knocked on the door and he told me to go away, that he was fine. He was in there a really long time. I thought he might have the flu or something. I took a phone call and then came back to check on him later. He was unconscious in his room. I called nine-one-one and got him to the emergency room, where they said he'd over-dosed."

"One of the packets had leaked. Or rup-tured."

She nodded. "He almost died."

"Why didn't you ever tell me?"

"You were working like crazy, your father was on a business trip and —" she held her hands up as though beseeching him to understand "— Neil swore me to secrecy. Said he'd never do it again. Begged me to think about Dad's heart. Said if your dad died because I told him about the drugs, it would be on my head."

She gave a sad smile. "I didn't let that last part sway me, but it did make me think." She swallowed hard. "I was very worried what this information might do to Paul." His mother twisted a napkin between her fingers, shredding it, piece by piece. "And Neil promised. Took my hands, looked me in the eye and promised."

"And you believed him?"

She nodded. "He was scared. Truly terri-fied when he found out how close he came to dying. He said he was done with that and he'd stay away from the people he was involved with."

"People like that don't just let you walk away."

She swiped a few stray tears. "I made him go to counseling. Told him I'd tell your dad if he didn't. Neil didn't like it, but he did it. I thought he was doing better." She flicked a glance at him and shoved the napkin pieces away. "I searched his room every day and never found anything else. He had that good job at the construction company. He was going all over the city working and he seemed happy enough. Every once in a while he'd get an out-of-town job. He was doing well. I thought."

School had never been Neil's strong point, and their parents hadn't pushed the issue when he'd dropped out to work full-time. As long as he was working, they were happy to let him live with them until he saved enough to go out on his own.

"Then one afternoon, he'd just come home from an out-of-town job. I checked the bathroom and found a little pouch of white powder. When I asked him about it, he took it and said it wasn't what I thought. He was just holding it for a friend." Tears clouded her blue eyes and she swallowed hard. "I'm not stupid, Jordan. I figured he was using again. He denied it, of course, but I knew."

"Oh, Mom, why didn't you say something?"

"I hadn't said anything to your father the first time. This time I was going to say something, and Neil knew it. He stormed out and I never saw him again." Her voice cracked on the last word. Jordan squeezed her fingers and she took a steadying breath. "He left to go on that trip to Mexico. I was trying to figure out how to tell your father before Neil came home. The next call we got was from Neil saying he was in jail, that he was being wrongly held. And then later, from the police saying he was dead."

"You kept that from me?"

Jordan and his mother swiveled as one to see his father standing in the doorway, face pale. The sick look in his eyes shouted his betrayal. Jordan's stomach sank.

His mother sighed and nodded. "I did. And before you say anything, I thought long and hard about it before I did it. I was scared your heart couldn't take it."

"Then we have a lot to talk about."

"I guess we do."

Jordan rose. "I'm sorry."

"Why did you decide to tell us this now?" his mother asked.

Before Jordan could answer, his father asked, "It's because of Katie Randall, isn't it?"

Jordan considered acting like he didn't

know what he was talking about, but couldn't do it. "Part of it's about her. I won't lie, I'm interested in dating her and getting to know her better." He paused and rubbed his eyes. "I've been debating whether to say anything to you since I read the autopsy report."

"Wish you'd said something before now," his dad said.

Jordan looked him in the eye. "No, you don't."

Tears filled his father's eyes, and he blinked them back. "I'm not sure I believe it."

"I know. It's hard to swallow." He glanced at his mother, who stared at her hands. "Talk to Mom. Work it out. Don't let Neil's death destroy you two. He may have been into some bad stuff, but he loved you guys." A sob broke from his mother's throat, but she nodded her agreement.

Jordan hugged each parent, letting them cling a little longer than usual. "I'm sorry." He couldn't seem to stop apologizing. Because he really was sorry. Sorry Neil had gotten into drugs. Sorry his mother had carried such a burden. Sorry his dad was feeling betrayed by his new knowledge. And sorry Neil was dead.

"Could we pray together?"

His mother's shaky question rattled him. Of course they needed to pray. He nodded and pulled his father to his feet. The man stood silent, refusing to say anything, but Jordan's mother gripped his hand and he didn't pull away. Jordan prayed from his heart, asking God's divine intervention in this painful way. And forgiveness for all involved.

"Amen."

"Amen," his mother whispered.

Jordan looked at his parents. "I was wondering if Katie could come in."

His mother looked startled. "What?"

"She's in the car."

"All this time, you've left her there?"

Jordan felt heat rise from his neck. "I needed to talk to you first."

"No." Jordan's father took a deep breath. "I'm not ready to see her."

"But Dad, I told you what happened. It's not Katie's fault."

"She still arrested him and put him in that cage with those animals." Stubborn pain glinted in the man's eyes and Jordan knew it might be hopeless to argue, but he had to try.

"Because Neil was driving drunk. He even took a swing at her. You're still in denial, Dad. You've got to realize that continuing to blame Katie for Neil's decisions isn't going let you heal. It's just going to keep your bitterness boiling until one day it's out of control and you have nothing left except that bitterness." Jordan knew he sounded harsh, but coddling his parents and handling them with kid gloves hadn't helped them move on. Still, he took a deep breath and softened his tone. "Think about it, Dad. You're going to grow into a bitter old man if you don't let this go."

His father jerked as though Jordan had reached out and punched him. He turned on his heel and left the room.

"Give us some time." His mother took a deep breath. "I have a feeling we're going to be talking a lot over the next several hours. Probably days."

Jordan nodded. Maybe she was right. Seeing Katie right now wouldn't be good. They both needed to process what they'd just learned about their dead son.

He gave his mom another hug. "Call me if you need to. I'll check on you later."

She nodded and Jordan headed for the front door, hoping Katie wasn't ready to kill him for making her wait so long.

FOURTEEN

Katie was ready to kill the man. She was sore all over and had a headache that wouldn't quit. Thankfully he'd left the car running with the heat on, or she'd be freezing, too. It was only the fact that she was warm that kept her from biting his head off when he slipped into the driver's seat and gripped the steering wheel.

Then she got a glimpse of the pain on his face, and her anger melted like ice cream on a hot summer day. She reached over and placed a hand over his. "Are you going to be okay?"

In one move he pulled her into a hug, burying his face in her neck. Stunned, she sat there, then wrapped her arms around his shoulders. A shudder went through him. "That was one of the hardest things I've ever done, but I'll be all right. I just pray they will be, too."

The need to comfort him swept over her

and she just let him cling to her in spite of the physical pain his embrace caused her.

He shifted to place lips over hers. A light kiss at first, as though he was saying thank you. She felt his deep sorrow, the tightly leashed control on his grief — and his unspoken need for comfort. She kissed him back and let time stand still.

When he lifted his head, he sighed and closed his eyes. "Thank you for being here."

Katie cleared her throat, trying to dislodge the lump of tears that had gathered. "Sure."

"They're not ready to see you yet."

"So you don't want me to go inside?"

"No. I think it's better if we let them digest everything I told them and try again another day."

She swallowed hard. "All right."

"Mom knew about Neil." The words sounded forced, painful. Then they registered.

"She knew?"

He nodded. "And she kept it from my dad. He's not happy with her."

"Oh, dear. I'm so sorry. Are they going to be all right?"

"I hope so."

He cranked the car and backed out of the carport. Katie touched his arm and pointed at his mother, who was walking toward them. He stopped the car in the driveway. "She's got something."

Jordan's mother approached the vehicle, carrying two cups with lids. Her smile was strained, but at least it was there. Jordan rolled the window down and she handed him the cups. "Hot apple cider."

Jordan passed one to Katie. Stunned, she took it. "Thank you, Mrs. Gray."

Jordan's mother bit her lip, then sighed. "You're welcome." Then she leaned in and pressed a kiss to her son's forehead. "Please be careful." She flicked a glance to Katie and once more offered a wobbly smile. "Goodbye."

"Bye."

Then she was back in the house and Katie was left staring at the front door. "Wow. Didn't expect that one."

"Tell me about it," Jordan murmured. But Katie could see the hope in his eyes and for the first time since Neil's death, she thought forgiveness might come from his parents.

Katie's phone rang as they pulled away from the house. She glanced at the number and did a double take. Her lieutenant. "This is Detective Randall."

"Katie, how are you feeling?"

"I'm sore and banged up, but nothing that will keep me down for long."

"Good, good, I'm glad to hear it. I was wondering when you plan to come back to work."

Katie swallowed. She'd planned to take advantage of every minute of leave she could get to work on Lucy's case, but . . . "I have four days of medical leave, but do you have something you need me to cover?"

"We're having a rash of crime here and I'm short staffed because of the flu. If you're able to help at all, I'd appreciate it. I'll give you some time off later. If the doc says no go, I understand. I don't want you to push it."

She was going to push it, whether it was working on Lucy's case or one he had for her. "Tell me what you need."

"I've got a dead body dumped off the highway along I-85 North. Gregory's already on his way. Can you meet him there?"

Katie bit her lip. She didn't want to be interrupted, but she knew she needed to do this for her boss. "I can be there in ten minutes."

"Thanks, Katie. I owe you."

"Sure." She hung up and looked at Jordan. "I need you to drop me off."

"Leave is up, huh?"

"Yes. For now. If I was truly incapacitated, it wouldn't be an issue, but I'm not."

"You'll be with your partner and a whole slew of other law enforcement personnel, right?"

"Right."

"It still may not be safe. I mean if he's got a sniper rifle —"

"Doesn't matter. I've got to do my job. I'm not going to let him take this from me, too. You can stay, if you want."

He narrowed his eyes as he thought, and at first she thought he might decide to stay. Then he shook his head. "You should be safe enough at the crime scene, and your buddies won't want me hanging around."

"We're not a territorial group." He scoffed, and she laughed. "Okay, okay. I wouldn't mind you there, but you might get a few looks from the others."

"I may go back to my office and look at the pictures from the neighborhood again."

"Call me if you come up with anything?"

"Absolutely."

Jordan dropped her at the crime scene, scoped out the area for the next twenty minutes, and when he didn't find anything or anyone that posed a danger to Katie, he headed for the office. He had an idea he wanted to implement.

Once in the office, he pulled Lucy's file and went straight for the pictures. He studied them one by one and gave a grunt of satisfaction when he thought he found what he was looking for. He picked up the phone and called Danny Jackson.

"Jackson here."

"Jordan Gray. I was wondering if you'd have a few minutes to talk about Lucy Randall."

A heavy sigh filtered through the line. "You still gnawing on that one like a dog with a bone, aren't you?"

"Yes, I guess I am."

"Then all right. But you gotta come to me. I'm down at McGee's Café."

Jordan grimaced. A thirty-minute drive. "All right. Don't leave, it'll take me half an hour to get there."

"I'm not going anywhere. Got nowhere to go."

Jordan gathered the photos and slid them back into the file. Then he grabbed his phone and sent a text to Katie, letting her know what he was doing. And begged her to stay with someone in order to ensure her safety until he got back.

She sent him a text assuring him she was surrounded by law enforcement and would let him know when she was finished. He tucked his phone into his pocket and sent up a prayer for her safety. And for God to bring closure to this search for Lucy — one way or another.

Fifteen

Katie did her best to keep her back from being exposed to any place she thought might be a good spot for a sniper to draw a bead on her. Out on the highway, trees lined the road for miles. Lots of hiding places. She noticed Gregory keeping an eye on her and the area around them, too. He said, "You all right?"

"I've been better, but I'm making it."

"Mom wanted to have flowers delivered, but you'd already been released. I told her to send them on to the hospital, you'd probably be back tomorrow."

She gave him a light punch on his arm. "You're hilarious." She pointed. "Who do we have here?"

He turned serious, all business now. "You're not going to believe it."

She lifted a brow. "Try me."

"It's Norman Rhames."

Katie gaped for a full two seconds, then

snapped her mouth shut. She rubbed her head and stared down at the body. "You're right. I don't believe it. I take it the lieutenant didn't know who he was when he sent me out here?"

"Nope. We just got confirmation on his identity about a minute before you drove up."

"I'll keep my hands off the investigation since there's a possible connection to Wray, but since I'm here, will you tell me what you know?"

"He was shot in the back of the head. Execution style."

Katie narrowed her eyes. "Now that's just shouting for an investigation. I want to know the connection between Norman Rhames and Wesley Wray."

Gregory pursed his lips. "You don't think it's a coincidence?"

"There's no way this is a coincidence."

He nodded. "I agree."

Katie got on her phone and called Jordan. He answered with, "Are you okay?"

In spite of the seriousness of the situation, Katie almost had to smile at his instant question. "What makes you ask that?"

"Cute."

"I'm also fine. Guess who our dead guy is?"

"Who?"

She filled him in. "You want to use your FBI contacts and see if you can find a connection between Wesley Wray and Norman Rhames sometime before Christmas?"

Katie felt a little disloyal to her department, but the FBI had more resources than a local department. With one phone call, Jordan would probably find what she wanted to know within the hour.

Her phone buzzed and she lifted a brow at the name that popped on the screen. "Hello, Detective Miller, what can I do for you?"

"You working that dead body on the highway?"

"I am."

"Heard it on the scanner. Thought you were on medical leave."

"I did, too."

He gave a half laugh, half snort. "Flu's swept through this department like a tsunami." He paused. "I got to thinking about your sister's case."

She stepped to the side out of the way of the crime scene unit that had just arrived. "Why's that?"

Gregory shot her a curious look that she ignored. She kept her back to a tree and let her gaze probe the area. Nothing set off her alarms. No rustling leaves, no shadowy figures. Nothing. Her muscles relaxed a fraction.

"Because you won't leave it alone and . . ." He paused.

"And?"

"And I might not have put some things in the notes that should have been there."

Her stomach knotted. "Why would you do that?"

"I didn't do it on purpose," he snapped. "I was going through a bad time that year. But that wasn't your sister's fault, and she deserved a better investigation than she got." He paused and she thought she heard him swallow. "If you'll meet me somewhere, I'll do my best to tell you everything I remember. I don't know if it'll do any good, but I'll tell you. And give you the notes that I made. I only have one copy and I don't want to fax them or email them anywhere. I don't want anyone stumbling across them."

The rough edge to his voice captured her attention one hundred percent. She looked around. "When and where can we meet?"

Another pause. "This can't get out, Katie. If it's known I didn't exactly do my job, my name will be mud around the department. No one will look at me the same. I don't want anyone to know we're meeting. This has to be completely confidential or it's going to come back to bite me."

"I won't say a word, Frank. I just want to find my sister." She stuffed down the anger she wanted to heap on this man's head. She couldn't blast him. Not yet. Not when he might have more information on Lucy. She looked around. "Give me another thirty minutes. Where do you want me to meet you?"

He gave her the address, and she memorized it. "I'll see you shortly."

Jordan pulled into the parking lot of the local pub. His buddy at Quantico had promised to get back to him within an hour with the connection between the two parolees. If he could find one. Jordan figured he would.

Katie sounded like she was fine, and Jordan offered up a prayer for the Lord to keep her that way.

He stepped inside the restaurant and spotted Danny Jackson at the bar nursing a drink and watching a football game on the television hanging from the wall. Jordan slipped onto the stool beside him. "Thanks for waiting for me."

"Like I said, I didn't have anywhere else to be. My wife died last year after a two-year battle with cancer, and I've just been going through the motions until I can join her."

"Sorry to hear that."

Danny shrugged. "I always thought I'd be the one to go first, you know?"

"Yeah. In our line of work, odds aren't exactly great for us to reach retirement age."

Danny grunted. "You didn't come here to chew the fat with me. What are your questions?"

Jordan didn't take offense at the man's gruffness; he figured that was just part of his personality. He'd seen too much, lived through some bad stuff and watched his wife die. The man had a right to be a little rough around the edges, he supposed. But he couldn't just let it go. "You think God's finished with you? That you don't have purpose anymore?"

Danny stilled. Then took a sip of the drink. "Funny you should say that."

"Why's that?"

"Because I was just wondering that very thing last night."

"So you believe in God?"

"More now than I used to. My wife was a believer." He shook his head. "She didn't want to leave me, but had no doubts where she was going when she took her last breath."

"I'm glad you can take comfort in that."

"I do. Not everyone can say the same for someone they've lost."

Jordan thought about Neil. While his brother had made some really rotten choices toward the end of his life, he'd given his heart to God at a middle school summer church camp. Jordan had no doubt that Neil was in heaven; he just wished he hadn't gone quite so soon.

He shoved thoughts of Neil away and focused on the man next to him. "But the Lord's left you here. Guess there might be a reason for that."

"Might be."

"And that reason might have something to do with Lucy Randall." He phrased it as a statement and waited.

A heavy sigh escaped the man and he rubbed a callused hand over his eyes. "It might."

Jordan took a stab in the dark. "Why don't you tell me what's been bothering you for the last fourteen years?"

Danny jerked like he'd been shot.

Bull's-eye.

Danny stared at him a minute, then finished his drink. "Come on."

"Where are we going?"

"To my truck, where we can't be overheard because the conversation we're getting ready to have never happened. Understand?"

"Gotcha."

Jordan followed Danny out to the man's oversized pickup truck. He had a fishing rod hanging on the gun rack on the back window of the king cab. Jordan climbed in the passenger seat and shut the door.

Danny cranked the truck and turned the heat on, but didn't move to put it in gear. "Ask me your questions."

"What is it you don't want to tell me? What are you afraid of?"

Danny barked a harsh laugh. "I'm not afraid of anything, son. Fear isn't keeping my mouth shut. Haven't you ever heard of a thing called loyalty?"

Jordan blinked. "Loyalty? To whom?"

Katie glanced at her watch and headed for her car. She was running later than she'd expected, especially with Gregory harassing her about needing an escort to wherever she was going.

She felt bad about putting him off, but she needed to talk to Frank, and Frank obviously didn't want an audience. If she had someone with her, he might clam up and she'd never learn what he wanted to tell her. However, she could let Jordan know what was going on. She shot him a text and waited for it to send.

Glancing around, she wondered if she was being watched, if someone planned on following her. With a shudder, she climbed into her vehicle.

If someone followed her, she and Frank would take care of it. Thirty-eight-year-old Norman Rhames hadn't had a chance. The medical examiner's off-the-record deduction had been that in all likelihood Rhames died from the gunshot to the back of his head. The lack of defensive wounds on his hands said he hadn't put up a fight. Katie wondered if he'd trusted whoever it was that had killed him.

Possibly.

But it wasn't the same person who'd killed Wesley Wray, because that had happened while the man was locked up.

She checked the area one last time. Gregory waved to her and stood watching with a frown on his face as she pulled from the gravel edge of the highway and merged with the traffic.

Nerves danced along the top of her skin and she kept her eye on the rearview mirror.

Jordan sat back as the answer hit him.

"Loyalty to your former partner. Frank Miller."

"Yeah. Frank."

"What was Frank's problem?"

Danny ran a hand over the gray stubble on his chin. "His problem was his personal life. More specifically, his wife and family."

Jordan nodded. "It happens."

"His wife was going to leave him. Gave him the whole line of grief about how he's always working and never home, yada yada."

"I feel for him. He sure didn't need that on top of the stress of the job." Jordan shook his head. Not every officer's wife felt that way, but too many of them did and those in law enforcement had a high rate of divorce.

Danny seemed to relax a fraction at Jordan's understanding words. "Well, she wasn't a prize when he married her, but she was a looker, and I guess that's what attracted him to her."

Jordan thought about Katie's beauty. While he appreciated the outward package, it was her heart and inner beauty that drew him like a magnet. "So Frank was a bit distracted from the investigation."

Danny nodded. "*Distracted* is a kind word. It was weird, too, because he pushed for the case. It had originally been assigned to two other detectives, but Frank wanted it. The

258

other detectives sure didn't care. As over-loaded as we all were, they gladly passed it on to us."

"Why was that?"

"He said he needed all the work he could get. Said he couldn't shut his brain off so he might as well do some good." Danny rubbed his chin. "And he did. He worked a ton of hours, slept at his desk, solved a lot of cases."

"But not Lucy Randall's."

"No. Not Lucy's." He frowned. "I'd never seen Frank so messed up. He finally told me what was going on. His wife had filed for divorce six months prior and then just four months before we got Lucy's case, his niece drowned at summer camp. Frank loved that little girl like she was his own. His sister and her husband had let him stay with them until he could get set financially, and he and Jenny really bonded during that time."

Danny took a swig of his drink and sighed. "He and his wife didn't have any kids, which turned out to be a good thing in the end. So not only was he struggling with the demise of his marriage, but his sister turned into a raving madwoman, wild with grief."

Jordan swallowed and pinched the bridge of his nose, his heart going out to the man.

"That's awful."

His phone vibrated, indicating a message. He'd check it in just a minute. He didn't want to do anything to cause Danny to clam up.

Danny said, "I told him to focus on the case, that if he just put all of his energy into solving Lucy's kidnapping, he could get his mind off of his troubles for a while."

"Did it work?"

"Seemed to. For a while." Danny chewed a toothpick and stared out the window.

"What else?"

A heavy sigh left the man. "We questioned a witness, and she talked about a car being at the scene."

"A gray sedan?"

Danny lifted a brow. "Yes. I documented it and put it in the report, then in the file. The next day it was gone. When I asked Frank about it, he just shrugged and said he didn't know what I was talking about. I documented it again and put it back in the file. A week later it was gone again. I demanded an explanation, and Frank dodged it. Said he didn't know and to quit bugging him about it."

"What'd you do?"

"I dropped it for the moment. We weren't getting anywhere on the case, anyway.

Didn't seem like a big deal."

Jordan pulled out the picture Mrs. McKinney had given him, then the ones taken the day of the kidnapping. "Take a look at this." He handed Danny Mrs. McKinney's picture. "This was shot a few days before Lucy was taken. The lady who took this picture spent a lot of time outside while the car was parked there. On this particular day, it was her son's birthday and they'd given him a skateboard. He was out there having a blast while his mom took pictures to put in her scrapbook." He handed him another picture. "This was taken by the crime scene photographer the day of the kidnapping."

Jordan tapped the photo. "This is one of the officers' vehicles. It's parked in the drive, but tell me that's not the same car in both pictures. The one on the street and the one in the drive."

Danny set them side by side and studied them for a full minute. "Yeah, they could be."

"The woman who took this picture said that the car behind the kid was parked there for hours at a time for two weeks. She even called the cops and they blew her off."

Danny looked at the pictures again. "It looks familiar." He swallowed hard. "That's a cop car."

"That's what I thought. I just want to know which cop was driving it."

His phone buzzed and he checked the caller ID. "I gotta take this. Why don't you see if you can pull the driver of that car from your memory."

Danny grimaced and Jordan turned his attention to the caller. "Seth, what do you have for me?"

"You wanted a connection between Mr. Wray and Mr. Rhames and I've got one for you."

Excitement quickened his pulse. "What is it?"

"The only connection I could find is that they have the same arresting officer."

Katie pulled into the parking lot of the warehouse and cut the engine of her rental. Gregory pulled in behind her and she rolled her eyes.

Katie slipped her phone into the back pocket of her jeans and walked up to Gregory. "What are you doing?"

"I was concerned." He crossed his arms and frowned down at her. "You wouldn't tell me where you were going. I was concerned."

"Look —" She had to get rid of him. If Frank showed up, he'd be mad as fire. And she might never learn what he knew about Lucy. "I need you to disappear for a while. I'm meeting a CI and I don't want you scaring him off."

"A confidential informant? For which case?"

"Which case do you think?"

The light went on for him. "Ah."

"Now go, will you?" She glanced at her watch. "He'll be here any minute."

"Are you sure? Let me stay as backup."

"I don't need backup with this one." She hesitated. "All right. But get out of sight, will you?"

Relief crossed his features. "Okay."

He left and Katie leaned against her vehicle. She checked her phone. No response from Jordan. That was weird. She texted him again.

A black sedan pulled into the parking lot. Frank pulled up beside her and climbed from his car.

"I guess this is as private a place as any," she said.

Frank shook his head. "Move your car out of sight. I'm going to do the same. I don't need someone saying they saw us meeting."

Katie sighed and dropped her arms. "Fine."

Once the vehicles were moved to Frank's

satisfaction, he said, "Let's go inside, I'm freezing."

Her phone buzzed and she pulled it from her pocket. Frank looked back. She said, "It's a text from Jordan wanting to know if I'm all right. We must have crossed texts."

"So tell him you're fine. You're a cop, Katie, and you act like you need a baby-sitter."

Katie's head shot up. "Someone's tried to kill me, Frank. Not once, but several times. Excuse me for appreciating friends who want to help look out for me."

Frank shrugged and entered the ware-house. Katie rolled her eyes and followed.

Jordan tucked his phone back into his pocket once he finished the call with Seth and checked for any messages from Katie.

Meeting a CI at warehouse on Buckley. Says he has info on Lucy. Will call when I'm done.

Satisfied she was still all right, Jordan processed what he'd just learned. Before he told Danny what Seth had just revealed, he wanted an answer from Danny. He pushed. "Whose car, Danny?"

"I can't say for sure."

"But it looks like . . ." He waited.

Danny slammed a fist on the steering wheel. "Frank's, all right? It looks like the car Frank and I used to drive."

Jordan pulled his phone back out and texted Katie, asking her who the CI was. Then he decided to forget the texting and dialed her number. When he got her voice mail, he said, "Frank knows more about Lucy's kidnapping than he's letting on. Be careful and let me know you got this message." He looked at Danny. "I just learned that Frank was one of the many arresting officers of Wesley Wray and Norman Rhames. Both of whom are dead."

"That's odd."

"Very. Everything is coming back to Frank Miller and I want to know why. Call him and tell him you need to meet him."

"No."

"Do it or you'll go down as an accessory."

"Accessory? Accessory to what?"

"Kidnapping."

"Kidnapping! He didn't take that girl. Sloppy police work maybe, but not kidnapping. You're crazy!"

Jordan leaned in. "I don't know if he took her or not, but I think he did." He shrugged. "Even if I'm wrong and he didn't take her, he covered up something in relation to it and you helped him. Now call him!"

Danny flexed his fingers on the wheel, then reached for the phone he'd tossed in the cup holder. He dialed the number.

"Put it on speaker."

"It's his number."

"Just put it on speaker and do it now."

Danny did. Frank's voice came on the line. As a message. "You know what to do." Beep.

Danny hung up.

Jordan sighed. "Call his office, please."

Danny dialed the number. Voice mail again.

Jordan pinched the bridge of his nose. "Will you show me where Frank lives?"

"Yeah. You want to follow me?"

"That would be great, if you won't try to lose me."

Danny shot him a perturbed look. "I won't." But he didn't move.

"What is it?"

"You really think Frank had something to do with that kidnapping?"

"It looks that way."

Danny swallowed hard and looked at the streetlight. "I thought he was just stressed out. He wouldn't have any reason to kidnap a kid. Where would he keep her?"

"Let's see if he's home. When we find him, we can ask him."

266

Jordan climbed out of the truck and into his vehicle. His mind centered on Katie and what her reaction would be if Jordan was right. He sent her another text asking her to call when she could, then pulled out onto the two-lane road to follow Danny.

Katie looked around. The warehouse had been empty for about four months. She remembered when this particular shoe business shut down. The machines still stood as though frozen in time. Or waiting for someone to start them up again.

Crates and boxes stacked to the ceiling had letters and numbers on them that probably meant something to the previous workers.

"Frank? You find anything?" She spun to look behind her, wondering where he'd gone.

A loud crack sounded and sparks flew from the nearest machine. Stunned, yet moving on reflex, Katie dove behind the nearest stack of crates. "Frank! Are you okay?"

Katie yanked her weapon and her phone. Fumbled the phone and watched it skitter under the crate. She dropped to her knees and shoved a hand after the device. Her fingers found it as another bullet pierced the wood about chest high.

"Frank! Frank, are you all right?"

When he didn't answer, Katie's blood ran cold. Had something happened to him? Was he lying hurt? But both shots had been in her direction. Had she been followed to the warehouse? With a smooth move, she slid the phone from under the crate and into her palm. She pressed 911.

The phone rang, then the call dropped.

"Stupid metal buildings," she muttered.

Her ears strained to hear the slightest noise that would indicate her attacker was near. She needed to move. She needed to find Frank.

"Katie, I'm over here."

Katie headed in the direction of his voice.

Sixteen

Jordan pulled to the curb behind Danny and climbed out of his car. Danny walked up to the door and rapped on it.

Nothing.

"Use your key," Jordan said. It was a wild guess, but one he was gratified to see paid off. Danny lifted a brow, then without another word, flipped the keys on his chain to the one that fit the door.

He pushed the door open and Jordan stepped inside. Neatness and order greeted him.

"I'm only doing this because if you're right, then I've been aiding a kidnapper all these years."

Jordan grunted. "You didn't know."

"I knew something was up, but I didn't bother to find out what."

True, the man had let things slide, but if he'd been aware of the real story, he would have probably done things differently.

And Lucy Randall might have grown up with her family.

Jordan pushed those thoughts aside and started looking for something . . . anything . . . that would give him a hint about what Frank had done with Lucy. "You going to help me search?"

"Yeah." The big man sighed and started down the hall. He disappeared into the first bedroom on the left.

Jordan searched the den, scoped the kitchen, then walked down the hall to the bedroom Frank had set up as an office.

A big executive-type desk sat against one wall with a leather chair pushed to the side, like Frank had just gotten up to get a cup of coffee and would be right back. His laptop screen saver flipped family pictures. Jordan jiggled the mouse.

The screen saver disappeared and a box popped up asking for a password.

Jordan left the computer and went for the drawers, checking his phone. No return text from Katie yet.

"You know if we find anything, it's not going to be admissible in court."

"I know. I'm not planning on taking anything, but Katie doesn't have enough for a search warrant yet." He paused. "I don't think. They might issue one based on the pictures of the cars, but I doubt it."

"I tried Frank's phone again. It went straight to voice mail."

Jordan opened the next drawer and pulled out a file labeled *Jenny*. "Who's Jenny?"

"His niece. The one who drowned."

Jordan opened the file and stared at the picture on top. "Danny, how old was Jenny when she died?"

"Seven. Or eight. I forget."

"Have you ever seen a picture of her?"

"Yes. He used to have a picture of her on his refrigerator and one on his desk. After she drowned, he removed all the pictures. Like it was just too painful for him to see them." He scratched his head. "I don't even remember what she looks like now."

Jordan flipped the picture over. "Her obituary's taped to the back." He turned back to the picture, then pulled out his cell phone and scrolled until he came to the picture of Lucy Randall. "Look at this."

Danny looked. And sucked in a deep breath. "They could pass for twins."

Jordan looked at Danny. "You think you could find the address of Frank's sister?"

"Probably."

Jordan's phone buzzed. Katie's answer, FRANK, sent fear exploding through him.

■ ■ ■ ■

Katie ducked as another shot came her way. "Frank!"

Chills of fear raced all over her. Frank was shooting at her.

She had to get out of the warehouse to get a cell signal or she was going to die.

She had to move, change locations. Find a better hiding place. *Something.* She took a deep breath and darted for the next stack of crates, expecting to feel the burn of a bullet entering her flesh. The shot came, but he missed. When he moved to get a better angle, she got a glimpse of him.

"Frank, stop! Why are you shooting at me?" She flipped her phone on silent.

"Because you keep sticking your nose where it doesn't belong!"

Lucy.

"She's my sister. Why don't you want me to find her?"

Another shot. She ducked, noticed she had one bar and punched in 911 on her cell phone again.

It rang once, twice. "Nine-one-one, what's your emergency?"

"I'm —"

The phone blipped the sound of the

dropped call and Katie bit back a groan. She quickly typed a text to Jordan, then one to Gregory. A footstep squeaked to her left. She caught her breath and moved toward the edge of the crates.

"Where's my sister? Where's Lucy?" she called and moved as silently as she could down a passageway made of crates toward the window to her right.

Another shot cracked the wood where she'd just been. But Frank wouldn't answer. She figured he was doing his best to hunt her down and didn't want to give away his location by opening his mouth. Fine. Two could play that game. She did her best to regulate her breathing, control the fear racing through her. If she could get to the window, maybe she could find a signal.

Jordan's phone beeped, indicating a text message. He read aloud, "Need help. Two-four-five-six Buckley. No signal." Terror shot straight through him.

Danny glanced at him and frowned. "Katie?"

"Yeah." Immediately, he dialed her number. Straight to voice mail.

"That doesn't sound good," Danny said.

Jordan punched in the number for Katie's partner. Gregory answered on the second ring. Jordan snapped, "Katie's in trouble." He gave the man the address.

Gregory said, "I got her text. I'm on the way. I just got a report about shots fired there."

Jordan punched a text back to her.

On the way.

A sick feeling engulfed him. *Please, God, let her be all right.*

Katie fired back in the direction the last shot had come from and thought she heard sirens in the distance. It was hard to tell. It might just be the ringing in her ears. She prayed it was sirens. Her nose itched. The smell of gunpowder filled the air and she had to hold her breath to ward off a sneeze.

A crate fell to her right and she spun, then darted toward it and to the right behind the crates next to it. Had Frank pushed one over trying to trap her into exposing her location? Or was it an accident?

Either way, she stayed put, breathing in through her nose and out through her mouth. She looked at her phone. Still not a good enough signal to make a phone call. The window was too far, with too much open space between her and it.

And where was Frank?

Another shot sent shards of wood raining down on her. One piece sliced the skin on the back of her hand and she bit her lip to keep from crying out. Blood dripped. Another hard piece grazed her forehead and she blinked as she hit the cement floor.

Come on, come on, where are you, Gregory? Jordan?

She couldn't hold Frank off forever. She scuttled toward what had once been a break area with a kitchen. The appliances were gone, but the granite countertops were still there, as well as the cement base they sat on.

Her phone vibrated. She glanced at the screen.

On the way.

Relief filled her. Blood dripped from her hand and she pressed it to her jeans, trying to stop the flow.

Gritting her teeth, she did her best to ignore the pain that bit at her. Her entire body still ached from all the trauma it had been through in the last few days. She'd pushed herself hard and was paying for it.

God, please. Don't let this man kill me.

Jordan led the way to the address Katie had texted him. When he pulled up, he flashed his FBI badge to the officer on crowd-control duty. Knowing a gunshot came from the warehouse, all he wanted to do was rush the place. Common sense and training held him still. Worry for Katie ate a hole in his belly.

Danny raced toward the doors, ignoring the shouts for him to stop. Jordan flashed his badge again and took off after the man. "Danny! Wait!"

Danny ignored him. He pulled open the door and stepped inside the warehouse. Jordan pulled his weapon as the SWAT team descended. He followed Danny inside and let the door close behind him.

"Frank!" Danny's voice held a desperation that made Jordan wince. "Frank, are you here?"

"Get out of here, Danny! This doesn't concern you." His voice echoed, but Jordan thought it originated from the left. He started moving in that direction, using the crates as shelter.

"There're cops all over the place," Danny called out. "They have evidence placing you at the kidnapping. I don't want you to die, and that's how this is going to end if you don't come out."

"Mind your own business, Danny."

"Why'd you do it, Frank? Why'd you take her?"

"Shut up! Just shut up!"

Jordan glanced around. Frank was hiding, but he had a good idea of where the man was. While Danny kept Frank's attention, Jordan slipped behind the nearest crate and stopped to listen.

Katie froze at the new voice. Danny Jackson. She moved to the left and found herself closer to the window. When Frank had answered Danny, his voice had been scary close. She backed up, stepping carefully, her goal no longer the window, but Frank.

Help was here. She needed to help them help her.

She turned, silent and watchful. Where was he? Her fingers gripped her weapon. The safety was off. Step by slow step, she moved.

A scuff from behind. She turned and came to an abrupt stop when a vise dropped over her head and closed around her throat. Adrenaline rushing, Katie dropped her phone, but years of training sent her into defense mode. She stepped backward into her attacker, jabbing with her elbow.

He deflected the blow and jammed his gun into her ribs. She gasped and stilled. Her heart beat with fear and anger.

"I took those courses, too, remember?" he hissed into her left ear.

"So what now, Frank? You know how this is going to play out. You either let me go or we're both going to wind up dead."

"I'm not ready to die yet."

"Then let me go."

"I'm not going to prison, either."

Terror curled in her belly.

"Frank!" Danny Jackson's voice again.

Frank stiffened and tightened his grip on her throat. She choked and he loosened it slightly. "Now we're going to walk out of here and get in the car and go."

"They'll just follow."

"Then we'll lose them."

"What did you do?" she whispered. "What did you have to do with her kidnapping? Why did you botch the investigation?"

Jordan could hear Katie's pained questions. Frank didn't answer her. He peered around the edge of the crates, could hear the negotiator on the megaphone. Frank didn't answer. In fact, he acted like there wasn't a whole city of cops outside the building.

He had a tight grip on Katie's throat, and Jordan could see the man's weapon pressed against her side. His heart thudded, and he took a deep breath. One shot. He'd only get one shot. He'd better make it count.

The SWAT team was useless without windows. If they couldn't see the perp, they couldn't shoot him.

"Frank, come on, man, talk to me."

Danny was in full cop mode, shrugging off his retirement like he'd never left. Jordan just prayed the man could talk some sense into his former partner while Jordan figured out a way to disarm Frank. Or shoot him.

"Frank! They've got evidence that you kidnapped Lucy Randall," Gregory joined in.

Jordan spun back and stepped around the crate so he could see the door. Gregory had slipped into the warehouse along with four SWAT members. He turned his attention back to Katie. She had gone perfectly still. "You? You kidnapped her?"

Whispered curses slipped from Frank's lips. "I had to."

To Jordan, it looked as though Frank's grip wasn't quite as tight. Everyone talking to him had distracted him.

Jordan raised his weapon and closed one eye as he centered the muzzle on Frank's lined forehead. But the man had a gun on Katie. If Jordan shot, would Frank's hand spasm and pull the trigger?

Frustration gripped him.

He shifted and tried to catch Katie's eye.

She saw him and her eyes widened.

Then she wilted straight to the floor, as though her legs had given out.

Frank cursed and held her by her chin. He looked up just as Jordan pulled the trigger.

SEVENTEEN

Katie felt Frank jerk and dropped the rest of the way to floor. She rolled and kicked out, clipping his knees and bringing him down beside her.

Before she could blink, Jordan was on the man and rolling him to his stomach, yanking his hands behind his back. "You're under arrest."

"You shot him. Oh, please tell me you didn't kill him," Katie said.

Frank groaned, and Katie felt a giddy shot of relief.

Jordan grunted as he clipped the cuffs onto Frank and hauled him to his feet. "I was going to, but figured we'd never find Lucy if I went with a head shot. You dropped at just the right time and I caught him in the shoulder. Nice moves."

"Thanks. Glad he didn't pull the trigger when I slumped." She stood in front of Frank and felt a strange mixture of emotions. And detachment. "Where's my sister?"

Frank shook his head and grimaced. The amount of blood covering his shirt said the shoulder wound probably needed to be looked at pretty fast.

Law enforcement had them surrounded. Gregory looked at her. "You all right?"

"I'm alive, so I guess that means I'm just fine."

He nodded. Katie waved paramedics over and Jordan helped Frank onto the gurney. None too gently, she noticed. Frank cried out and sucked air between his clenched teeth.

Katie noticed Danny Jackson staring at Frank. When he saw her watching, he shook his head. "I didn't know, I promise."

Katie stepped up to the gurney and looked down at the man who'd ripped her family apart. "Why?"

He opened his eyes and glared. "It doesn't matter now, does it?"

"Of course it matters!" Her fist balled and she was ready to slug him. "Where is she? Is she alive?" The question ripped from her. Frank looked away and Katie grabbed his good shoulder and shook it. He gasped. "Is she alive!"

He met her gaze. "No. She's not."

Her knees buckled, and she felt Jordan's hands catch her on her way to the concrete. "No. No, no, no. Please . . ."

Jordan helped her back to her feet and away from Frank. She couldn't stop the sobs that choked her. Jordan held her, then shook her. Why wouldn't he just let her give in and have a moment of grief?

"Katie! Listen to me!"

She hiccupped and shuddered. "What!"

"I don't think she's dead."

Katie drew in a ragged breath and stared. "Why?"

"Because of what we found at his house."

"You searched his house?"

"Yeah. And now that we got him on all kinds of charges including attempted murder, we won't have any trouble getting a search warrant."

Katie wiped her eyes and sniffed. "What'd you find?" She watched the ambulance pull away from the parking lot.

"Evidence that he took Lucy." He gripped her hands. "His niece died a few months before Lucy was snatched. Danny talked about how inconsolable the family was and how Frank nearly fell apart, but that the job was the only thing that kept him going."

"So he took Lucy as an attempt to replace his niece?"

"That's what we think."

"So where is she?"

"I'm going to take a wild guess and say he took her and gave her to his sister."

"Where do they live? Let's go."

Jordan checked his phone. "I've got her address right here." He placed a hand on her arm to stop her from heading to the car. "Let me call and see if she's home." He looked around. "Plus, you're not done here."

Katie took another breath and closed her eyes. She had to get herself together. Hope flared like a spotlight, bright and piercing. Lucy might be alive. If she was, she'd just celebrated her twenty-first birthday two weeks ago. And she might even be somewhere close by. Her fingers itched to pick up the phone and call her parents, but she couldn't do that until she knew for sure. She wouldn't dare take a chance on raising their hopes only to have them dashed.

It seemed to take forever, but Katie managed to get through the wrap of the crime scene, giving her statement and chugging a bottle of water.

Impatience zipped through her. She looked at Jordan. "Are you ready?"

"She apparently still lives with her par—" He shot her a look. "The family that she

—" He held his hands up.

Katie bit her lip. "I guess they're her parents now, aren't they?"

Jordan nodded. "I'm sorry. I know this is a hard one, but she's lived with them for fourteen years. If they raised her as their own, then yes, she probably thinks of them as her parents."

"Okay. I know you're right. I'll just have to remember that." She paused. "In fact, we probably should talk to her parents first and ask them the best way to approach telling Lucy the truth about her past."

Jordan pressed the phone to his ear. "She's not answering her phone."

"Then I'll sit outside her house until someone comes home."

The four-hour drive to Raleigh, North Carolina, passed mostly in silence broken by Katie's phone calls to the Banks residence every thirty minutes.

Katie was glad for Jordan's company. He drove to the address he'd gotten from his buddy at Quantico. Bill and Lindsay Banks lived in an older middle-class neighborhood with a lot of ranch-style houses on one-acre lots. The Banks' still hadn't answered when Jordan pulled to the curb of the house.

Katie's phone rang, and she glanced at

the ID, then at him. "It's my parents' number."

"Go ahead and answer it. We're just going to be doing a waiting game for the next little while. I'll step out of the car and give you some privacy if you want."

Katie shook her head and clicked the phone off. "No. I don't want to talk to them yet. I want to be able to tell them I found Lucy and when they can see her."

"You think finding Lucy is going to make your mother love you again?" He asked the question softly and she winced. He grimaced. "Never mind. I'm sorry."

"No," she said, her voice low. "It's a valid question. The answer is — I don't know."

"But you keep trying."

She gave a sad smile. "I don't know how to stop at this point." She took a deep breath. "However, I do think I'm going to have to come to terms with the fact that my mother may never change, and I'm going to have to figure out a way to accept that."

"And forgive yourself for Lucy's kidnapping?"

Another wince. "Yes." She shot him a look. "Just like you need to forgive yourself for the death of that little girl."

Jordan's fingers flexed on the steering wheel. "I know it wasn't my fault. In my

286

head I know that."

"I understand. I've finally come to see that Lucy's kidnapping wasn't my fault. I didn't cause it. Someone else chose to do that and blaming myself is exactly the wrong thing to do. God doesn't blame me. My mother may blame me, but God doesn't, and that's what I have to get through to my heart."

"You've been doing a lot of thinking."

"I have." She gripped his hand. "Jordan, that little girl's death wasn't your fault. God doesn't blame you."

His throat worked and he nodded. "I'm starting to see that." He glanced at her. "Thanks to you."

Her phone rang and she jerked. "My dad again."

"Answer him, Katie. Talk to him."

With a deep sigh, Katie pressed the button. "Hello?"

"Hi, Katie, I hope this is a good time." Her mother's voice echoed in her head. For a moment, shock held Katie speechless. Her mother had called her.

She cleared her throat. "Hi, Mom. I have time. What can I do for you?"

After a slight hesitation, her mother said, "I wanted to know if you'd like to come to lunch on Sunday."

Katie felt tears spring to her eyes. "I would

love to, but —" She bit her lip. No sense in pushing things too soon. She'd ask her father about her mother's out-of-character behavior later.

"But why am I calling?"

"It doesn't matter. I'm just glad you did." She swallowed hard against another rush of tears.

"It does matter and maybe this isn't the time or the way to handle it, but to put it bluntly, I'm tired of being afraid."

"What?"

Her mother cleared her throat. "Your father told me what happened with you. How someone threatened to hurt you if you didn't stop looking for Lucy." A sob and then a shaky breath filtered through. "And it was like a slap in the face. Since the day you decided to become a cop, I've been preparing myself to lose you, too. When your father told me what you were going through, with the fire, then the car wreck, it was a wake-up call. I've been consumed by fear and I refuse to live that way any longer. And I needed to tell you."

Katie sat stunned, unable to think, breathe, move. She finally let out a small gasp.

"I owe you an apology, Katie, and I didn't want to tell you this over the phone, but I didn't want to wait another minute, either. I love you and I'm so sorry for not being the mother you needed."

Tears rolled down Katie's cheeks. How long had she waited to hear those words? A car pulled into the Banks' driveway and Katie sucked in a deep breath.

"I love you, too, Mom. Thank you for calling and telling me. I needed to hear it."

They hung up with promises to get together soon. Katie looked at Jordan, still in shock. "Did that just happen?"

"Sounds like it."

"Could you hear?"

A light flush highlighted his cheeks. "Sorry, but yes. Every word."

"She loves me," Katie whispered. "I did all I could to earn her love, but she didn't care about all that stuff."

"You can't earn love, Katie. And I think that's a hard lesson for all of us to learn sometimes. Love is a gift and you can't earn a gift."

"Ephesians two, verse eight," she whispered.

"What does it say?"

" 'For by grace you have been saved through faith, and that not of yourselves; it is the gift of God.' " Katie lifted her eyes to his. "She just offered me the gift of her love, a love I was trying so hard to earn, and I'm about to explode."

Jordan reached out and placed a hand under her chin. Her eyes met his very intense and direct gaze. "What's not to love?" he asked softly.

Katie wondered if she'd ever be able to draw a deep breath again. Her heart felt too full. Like it had grown several sizes and was squeezing her lungs. "What are you saying?"

"I'm saying . . . we have a lot to talk about. After you figure out if your sister is here."

Katie almost started laughing at the timing of everything. Instead, she gave a hiccupping sniff and took the tissue Jordan handed to her. "Let me get myself cleaned up and then we can go in." She mopped and scrubbed, then inspected the damage in the visor mirror. "It's a good thing I don't normally wear makeup," she muttered.

Jordan smiled and opened his door. "Ready?"

"As I'll ever be."

She climbed out of the car and walked toward the house.

Jordan took a deep breath as he stood beside Katie and watched her rap on the front door. This was it. They had no idea if

Lucy was here or not. But someone was home.

Footsteps sounded and then they were face-to-face with a woman in her late forties. Jordan thought about the profile Seth had sent him. One he'd had to skim fast. But he recognized Lindsay Banks.

Katie smiled. A quick twitch of her lips. "I'm Katie Randall. I was wondering if I could have a moment of your time."

"What's this about?"

"It's about your daughter."

"Lucy?"

"Um . . . yes, ma'am. Lucy." Jordan heard her choke on the name, but she forced it out.

"Is she all right?" Stark terror stood out in the woman's eyes.

Jordan said, "She's just fine as far as we know, but we have some information we need to share with you. Is she here?"

"No. She's at work."

Jordan could tell they were scaring the poor woman to death. Katie apparently sensed it, too. "Mrs. Banks, could we just come in and sit down?"

"I'm sorry, I don't let strangers in my house."

Katie sighed and flicked a look at Jordan. She pulled out her badge and showed it to the woman. Mrs. Banks sucked in a deep breath and pressed a hand to her lips. "Do I need to call my husband?"

"If you'd like to. He needs to hear this, too." It might be better to have both of them there. Were they in on the kidnapping? Did they know what Frank had been up to? Her gut said no, Frank acted on his own, but Katie wanted to know that for sure.

Mrs. Banks stepped back and opened the door. Jordan followed Katie and the woman into a formal living area. She gestured to the couch, but didn't sit. Katie took one end of the sofa and Jordan slid into one of the straight-backed wooden chairs. He figured Mrs. Banks would feel better without him looming over her.

She crossed her arms and let her gaze swing back and forth between them. "Now, what's this all about? Is Lucy in trouble?"

"Not at all," Jordan said. "Are you going to call your husband?"

She hesitated. "Tell me what this is about first."

Katie ran a hand through her hair and sent up a silent prayer for the right words. "Mrs. Banks, we know you lost a daughter when she was seven years old."

The woman's eyes went wide and she sank into the nearest chair. "Yes. That's right."

"And we know soon after that you took in a young girl about the same age."

"Yes. Lucy. Her parents were killed in a fire and there were no other living relatives." She gave a small laugh and rubbed her head. "It's just amazing how it all happened, really. I was grieving for Jenny." Her eyes teared up. "I still do, but —" a tremulous smile curved her lips "— my brother, Frank, is a detective in Spartanburg. Frank appeared on my doorstep with little Lucy, saying she needed a home. When I saw her, I couldn't say no." She sighed. "She saved my life." She twisted her fingers. "You see, I couldn't have any more children after Jenny, so . . . she was my world and when she died . . ."

Katie reached over and patted the woman's hand. "I'm so sorry, Mrs. Banks. I can't imagine how awful that was for you and Mr. Banks."

Katie had a sneaking suspicion that the Banks' had no idea that Frank had kidnapped Lucy. "Did you not see news reports on Lucy? I know she made CNN and other major news networks."

Mrs. Banks grimaced. "We don't watch the news. Too depressing."

A fact Frank would have known.

Mrs. Banks closed her eyes. "I don't talk

about Jenny's death very much, simply because it was a horrible time." When she opened her eyes, her grief faded and she smiled. "But Lucy was —" She paused. "Lucy was our gift straight from God."

Eighteen

Katie cleared her throat, but the knot that had developed refused to budge. She talked around it. "Mrs. Banks, we have reason to believe that your Lucy is really Lucy Randall."

The woman's forehead creased. "Who's that?"

"A young girl who was taken from her home fourteen years ago."

"Taken." Mrs. Banks gaped. "And you think —"

"Ma'am, I know this is hard to process, but we have evidence that Frank Miller kidnapped Lucy Randall and gave her to you."

Jordan's soft words filled the room.

"Evidence?" she whispered. "No. Oh, no, please . . ."

"Would you like to call your husband? There's more."

With a shaky hand, Mrs. Banks pulled a

cell phone from her jeans pocket and dialed a number. "Bill, there's a bit of an emergency at home. I need you to come." She listened. "No. I'm not hurt. Just come and drive carefully. You don't need to speed." She hung up and looked at Katie, then Jordan. "What's this evidence?"

Katie exchanged a glance with Jordan and decided to just be honest. "Frank's been arrested for murder and attempted murder. We have someone who puts his unmarked car at the scene of the kidnapping, and he basically admitted to taking her."

The woman's face went a pale gray. Katie had to contain herself from demanding Mrs. Banks get on the phone and call Lucy and tell her to come home. First she had to help these people deal with this shock. Then she could see Lucy.

"Frank? Arrested?" She sounded dazed.

Katie bit her lip. The news was too much. She should have had Mrs. Banks call her husband right away. She slid over and took the woman's hand. "We'll wait for your husband to get here to finish this."

She nodded and for the next twenty minutes, they sat. Just when Katie thought she couldn't bear the silence a minute longer, the front door opened and Mr. Banks bolted into the house. "Linds? Where are you?"

"Here, Bill." Mrs. Banks stood and her husband whirled. His salt-and-pepper hair was askew, as though he'd run his hands through it repeatedly on the drive home. "What is it? What's wrong?"

"They think Lucy is —" She couldn't say another word as sobs overtook her.

Bill Banks looked at Katie and Jordan. Katie introduced herself and began the story once more.

When she finished, the couple simply stared at her in shock.

"So you're saying my birth family is still alive?" A soft voice from the dining room grabbed their attention. Katie jumped to her feet.

Mrs. Banks cried out. "How much did you hear?"

"All of it. Daddy called and said there was something wrong at home and he wasn't sure what, but it sounded serious. I came right here. I heard you talking and didn't want to interrupt and —" she spread her hands "— I heard everything."

Katie stared at the young woman. A stranger and yet . . . familiar, too. "Lucy," she whispered.

Lucy looked at her. "So I was kidnapped?" She stared at her parents. "You told me they were dead. That they all died." She wrinkled her brow. "I remember them, you know. In snatches and bits and pieces, but I remember them."

Mrs. Banks sobbed against her husband's shoulder.

Katie sucked in a deep breath. "Lucy, what do you remember about that day?"

"He took me from the yard. He was very nice, but very firm. He was a police officer and told me I had to go with him. So I did." She swiped a hand through her hair. "He became my uncle. Uncle Frank. I remember being sad and missing my family. My sister. Katie." She whispered the name, and Katie bit back a sob.

"That's me. I'm Katie," she said softly.

Lucy's brow rose and her eyes narrowed as horror entered them. "You're my sister?"

"Yes."

"I was kidnapped."

Katie nodded. "And I've been looking for you ever since."

Lucy's gaze flew from Katie to Jordan to her parents and back to Katie. "I need to sit down."

She slid to the sofa next to her mother, and Katie restrained herself from reaching out and touching the girl. Lucy hugged her mother, then crossed the room to her father and wrapped him in a tight hug. She looked at Katie. "I want to see your evidence. If what you say is true, I want to know beyond a shadow of a doubt."

Katie nodded. It seemed to be all she could do.

Tears in her eyes, Lucy smiled, then moved to wrap Katie in a tight hug. "I've missed you."

Katie let a sob slip out as she hugged her sister back. "And oh, how I've missed you."

Lucy drew in a deep breath and looked at her parents. Katie followed her gaze. They looked shell-shocked. Katie knew what she had to do. She looked at her sister. "Take your time and reassure them, then call me." She pulled a card from her pocket and slid it in her sister's hand.

Lucy's tears spilled over, but she simply nodded as Katie turned to leave.

Jordan slipped his hand over hers and gave her a squeeze. She squeezed back and made it out the door and into the car before she turned, wrapped her arms around his neck and cried her happiness into his shoulder.

And bless the man, he let her do it.

After about ten minutes, he started mopping her face with a tissue. "Come on, Katie, I'm going to need an oar to steer the car if you keep this up."

She sniffed and sat away from him, taking the tissue and finishing the job. "I'm sorry, I'm just so happy and almost unwilling to believe it's true. We found her."

He handed her a bottle of water. She eyed it suspiciously. "How long has this been in here?"

He laughed. "Since last night. It won't kill you, I promise."

She took a swig and sighed. "I need to call my parents."

"Yes."

Katie took out her phone and dialed her parents' number. Her mother answered on the second ring. "Hi, Mom. I've got some news for you."

"News? What kind of news?"

"We found Lucy."

EPILOGUE

Katie looked around the dinner table. Christmas Day had arrived with snow flurries and cold temperatures, but inside her parents' warm house, Katie marveled at her mother's bright eyes and happy smile. She kept coming back to the sight of Lucy sitting between her birth parents, with the parents who'd raised her sitting across the table.

Jordan sat to her right. And wonder of wonders, his parents had agreed to join them. His father wasn't falling over himself to be pleasant to Katie, but at least he could be in the same room and not cast blame.

Jordan said his parents had spent many hours working out the fact that his mother had chosen to keep Neil's secret. They were going to counseling to deal with everything, including accepting that Katie didn't deserve Paul's blame. And he was beginning to see the light.

Katie just shook her head. Never in a million years would she have pictured this scene. And yet here they all were.

Tears threatened and she rose on the pretense of carrying some empty dishes into the kitchen.

Jordan followed her. She put the dishes into the sink and felt his hands fall on her shoulders. He turned her to face him. "All you all right?"

She looked up into his eyes and felt her heart kick into overdrive. "I'm more than all right. I don't have the words to describe how I feel right now. I feel overwhelmed with how everything worked out." A tear slipped down her cheek and he brushed it away. "This isn't the normal ending to a kidnapping." She blinked. "I really believed she was dead, Jordan."

"I know. I did, too."

"And I keep having trouble wrapping my mind around the fact that we found her."

"I know."

"You know how Lucy's other mother said that Lucy was her gift from God? Well, reuniting our family is another gift."

"God's done some amazing work over the last few weeks. One of those things was keeping you alive to enjoy this moment." He pulled her to him and buried his face in her neck. "I don't know what I would have done if you'd been killed."

She pushed him back and cupped his cheeks with her palms. "I think I love you, Jordan."

He blinked, then gave a laugh and grabbed her around the waist to lift her so they were nose to nose. "I know I love you, silly woman."

He kissed her, a long, thorough kiss that left her breathless. She grinned. "I'm so thankful God sent me to Finding the Lost."

"Will you marry me?"

She gaped. "Marry you?"

"What? Too soon?"

"No. Yes. Maybe. No."

He grinned. "So which one do I pick?"

She laughed through her tears. "Yes."

"Soon?"

"Soon."

"Awesome."

He planted another kiss on her lips, and she clung to the happiness and blessings God had chosen to bestow upon them.

She pulled back. "Not every day is going to be this wonderful, you know."

"I know, but let's enjoy while it lasts."

"I'm good with that."

She kissed him again, knowing her future was bright and God's love was enough to get them through whatever came their way. God's unconditional love. A love she couldn't earn, but which was freely given.

A love she accepted with a grateful heart. A love she planned to pass down to her children and her children's children. Children. The thought made her weepy again. Oh, yeah, she wanted children. Jordan's children.

Jordan pulled back and kissed her nose. "Merry Christmas, Katie."

"Merry Christmas, Jordan."

Dear Reader,

Thank you so much for joining me on this journey, not just to find Lucy, but to discover the unconditional love of an amazing God and His free gift of eternal life to those who would accept it. I'm so glad His love is something I can't earn. Why? Because I could never do enough to earn a love like that. Having to earn God's love is a setup for failure. Just like Katie couldn't earn her mother's love, we can't earn God's. Katie had the choice to accept her mother's love in the end — or reject it — and she chose to accept it. As a result, it set her free in an emotional sense. God's love sets us free from death. I pray you now have this love and have accepted His priceless gift.

Again, I hope you enjoyed the story and drew closer to God as a result of reading it. I love to hear from my readers. Feel free to find me on the internet at www.lynette eason.com and sign up with my newsletter if you'd like to be notified of upcoming dates for my books to be released. I'm also on Facebook at www.facebook.com/lynette .eason and Twitter @lynetteeason. God bless you and until next time,

Lynette Eason

QUESTIONS FOR DISCUSSION

1. Katie Randall's little sister disappeared from their front yard fourteen years ago. She has blamed herself ever since. Do you think she was irresponsible in leaving her sister to help her neighbor? Have you made a mistake in your past that had serious consequences you still blame yourself for?

2. Jordan Gray only works cold cases. He has his own past mistakes to overcome and forgive himself for. He feels like it's his fault a child died, which is why he no longer works current abductions for the FBI. He joins Finding the Lost and meets Katie. Do you think the timing is coincidental, or do you think God sometimes places people in our lives at just the right time for a specific purpose?

3. Katie has dedicated her life to finding her

sister. She feels like she is unworthy to have happiness until her sister is found. Is there something you're so passionate about that you would put your life on hold to "fix" it?

4. Jordan is attracted to Katie, but his parents blame her for Neil's death. He doesn't want to do anything to upset his parents, so he has to fight his attraction for Katie. Have you ever been in a situation where you didn't want to hurt someone so you put your own feelings aside?

5. More than anything, Katie wants to be loved. Why do you think she feels the way she feels?

6. Katie does her best to earn her mother's love and each time she does something her mother still doesn't love her. It's like being rejected over and over. If you were in Katie's shoes, would you keep trying or would you give up? Why?

7. What is your favorite scene in this story?

8. Who is your favorite character in the story?

9. Detective Frank Miller was going through a very hard time, with his marriage crumbling and his niece dying. He made a decision to kidnap a child in order to save his sister's life and pull her out of her depression. What did you think about Frank after you found out his reasons for taking Lucy? Did you feel sorry for him at all? Why or why not?

10. Were you surprised Katie's sister, Lucy, was still alive?

11. When Katie finally finds her sister and has to tell her sister's "parents" that they have "adopted" a kidnapped child, they are devastated. Did you feel compassion for this couple? Why or why not?

12. Katie finally realizes that she can't earn her mother's love any more than we can earn God's love. We will never be good enough or do enough right things to make God love us. He chose to love us so much that He sent His son to die for us. Katie's mother finally tells her why she pushed her away for so long and tells Katie she loves her. Her mother's confession and subsequent offer of love frees Katie up so much. But what if Katie's mother hadn't

come around? What if Katie had to go through the rest of her life without her mother's love? Do you think she would have found peace at some point? Especially with Jordan by her side?

13. Jordan's mother kept her knowledge about Neil from her husband because she was scared it would bring on another heart attack. Do you think her reasons were valid? That she did the right thing? Or do you think she should have told him? (Remember, she just lost her son, and losing her husband because she told him the truth about Neil would have destroyed her.) What would you have done in her shoes?

14. What about Jordan? Should he have kept the truth about Neil's activities from his parents? Do you think letting them, most specifically his father, believe that Neil was wrongly arrested was the right thing to do? To spare their feelings? Or do you think it prevented their healing?

15. Were you surprised by who the villain was? If so, who did you think was the bad guy?

ABOUT THE AUTHOR

Lynette Eason makes her home in South Carolina with her husband and two children. Lynette has taught in many areas of education over the past ten years and is very happy to make the transition from teaching school to teaching at writers' conferences. She is a member of RWA (Romance Writers of America), FHL (Faith, Hope, & Love) and ACFW (American Christian Fiction Writers). She is often found online and loves to talk writing with anyone who will listen. You can find her at www.facebook.com/lynetteeasonauthor or www.lynetteeason.com.